YOU'V

Nick Warbur
teacher for t
become a full-
plays for stage and radio, including *Moonfleet* and *Conversations from the Engine Room*, which won the 1985 *Radio Times* Drama Award. For older children, he has written the novels *The Thirteenth Owl*, *The Battle of Baked Bean Alley*, *Normal Nesbitt*, *To Trust a Soldier* and *Ackford's Monster*, as well as a story for younger readers, *Dennis Dipp on Gilbert's Pond*. A Visiting Fellow of Chichester Institute of Higher Education, he is married with a son and lives in Cambridge.

Books by the same author

Ackford's Monster

The Battle of Baked Bean Alley

Normal Nesbitt, The Abnormally Average Boy

To Trust a Soldier

YOU'VE BEEN NOODLED!

NICK WARBURTON

For Dave and Elaine

First published 1998 by Walker Books Ltd
87 Vauxhall Walk, London SE11 5HJ

This edition published 1998

2 4 6 8 10 9 7 5 3 1

This book has been typeset in Sabon.

Printed in England
by Cox & Wyman Ltd, Reading, Berkshire

British Library Cataloguing in Publication Data.
A catalogue record for this book is available
from the British Library.

ISBN 0-7445-6049-7

CONTENTS

ONLY ON WEDNESDAYS

That January, near the beginning of term, someone left a pair of swimming trunks to dry on the radiator in the Humanities Room. Graham Keefe found himself sitting next to them in PSE. He tried to ignore them but they were hard to ignore. They were brightly coloured – at first he thought they were a bonnet, cast aside by some trendy baby – and they were steaming slightly. Every time Graham moved his head they flashed in the corner of his eye, and every time he breathed he inhaled a mixture of stale swimming pool and body odour. It became very hard to concentrate on PSE.

"This isn't healthy," he whispered to Nathan. "We shouldn't be made to breathe in a room like this."

"You don't have to breathe," Nathan said. "There's no rule about it."

"But we could get some kind of disease, breathing in trunk fumes. I mean, we don't know who they belong to. They could be Spader's or someone's..."

"Have you got a problem, Graham?" said Miss Garden, suddenly slapping a book on her desk.

"Well..."

"Because, if you have, I might be able to help you."

"As a matter of fact..."

"Which is what I'm here for, after all. Something to do with government, is it?"

"Government, miss?"

"The government of the country, Graham ... what we were just talking about."

She paused and they stared at each other blankly for a moment.

"The United Kingdom," she explained.

"Oh," said Graham, "the UK. I see. Yes – I mean no."

"No?"

"I haven't got a problem with government, miss, no..."

"I am so pleased. Perhaps we can carry on."

"But I have got a problem, miss."

"Yeah," said Angela Carr. "He's a nerd."

The others laughed but Graham ignored them.

"It's not the government, miss. It's the atmosphere."

"The atmosphere? What's wrong with the atmosphere?"

"It's not healthy. Sitting by the radiator with wet trunks..."

"Wet trunks? Have you been swimming?"

"No, miss."

"Then what have you...?"

Miss Garden cut her question short. It was probably best not to ask, she thought.

"They're steaming, miss. On the radiator."

"You've put your wet pants on the radiator?"

The others laughed again. They were beginning to wake up and take an interest.

"Trunks, miss, trunks," sighed Graham. "And they're not mine. I think they might be Spader's."

Miss Garden blinked at him. For a second she considered abandoning the conversation, but it had unsettled her. There was a mystery behind it and she wanted to know.

"What are you doing with Alex Spader's swimming trunks?" she asked.

"Nothing. They're nothing to do with me. But they're steaming, see, and it's getting into the atmosphere and..."

Miss Garden closed her eyes and put up a hand to stop him.

"No," she said. "This is not important. Can we forget it? Please."

"I've been trying to forget it, miss," Graham

went on, "but it's very difficult. I mean, I have to breathe and…"

"No, Graham. You're perfectly safe, believe me. I am fully trained. I have read and studied. No one in the history of humanity ever died from inhaling the fumes of wet swimming trunks."

And that might have been the end of it, had not Peter Smith decided to join in.

"Actually, miss," he said, "you can't know that."

Peter Smith was a smallish, neat boy. His smallness and his neatness – and the fact that he had such a sensible name – persuaded some people that he was devoted to study. In fact, he studied very little, except, perhaps, cookery, which was the only thing he took seriously. You wouldn't think so to look at him, but he was considered by many to be an artist among cake-makers. Miss Garden turned to him with a smile.

"Can't know what, Peter?" she said.

"That no one's ever died from breathing in Spader's trunk fumes. They might've done, in the mists of history, miss. Only it never got written down."

"It never got written down, Peter, because it didn't happen."

"Maybe not with these actual trunks, I grant you that. But some other trunks, at some other time. 1665, for instance."

"1665?"

"The Great Plague. A pair of trunks on a radiator in those days might've been really deadly. I mean, they blame rats and stuff but it could just as easily have been trunks, when you come to think of it."

"Don't be stupid," said Graham. "They didn't have radiators then."

"Or trunks, I bet," said Nathan, thoughtfully.

"Now listen..." began Miss Garden.

"Well, they wouldn't swim with nothing on," said Peter Smith, turning to appeal to the others. "Especially in the Thames, the middle of London. Nakedness was an abomination in those days, miss. Pardon my language. You could be arrested for it, and then you'd be in deep bother. You could find yourself in the care of one of Keefe's ancestors."

"How so?" asked Miss Garden.

"His dad's a screw, isn't he?"

"A screw? What are you talking about? You mean, he's a carpenter?"

"No, no, miss," chipped in Angela. "A screw. A warder at the prison."

"Leave my dad out of this, will you?" said Graham, blushing.

"But he is a screw ..." Smith went on.

"A prison officer."

"... so someone like him would lock you up for dipping naked in the Thames. It makes sense."

"No, it doesn't," said Miss Garden. "It makes no sense at all."

"It does, though, miss. Think about it. You go for a quick dip in the Thames. You hang your trunks by the fire, your servant walks by half an hour later, takes a deep breath and wham! Down he goes with the Great Plague."

"No, he doesn't."

"But you don't *know*, miss, do you? This is my point..."

"Shut up."

"No, really..."

"Shut up, Peter. We are talking about government."

"All right, then, government. The cabinet is having a meeting, say, and one of them comes in a bit late because..."

"No."

"But this is PSE in a way, isn't it?"

Miss Garden narrowed her eyes.

"How?" she said. "How is it PSE?"

"Because it's part of the unknown, isn't it? And that means religion, and religion comes into PSE. You can't know, but you could believe. Like God."

"I think I missed something somewhere," said Nathan. "How did God come into it?"

"It doesn't matter, Nathan. God doesn't come into it and we are about to change the subject."

"But, miss..."

"No, Peter. End of discussion."

"Well, all right, but I'm surprised at you, to be honest. You said we should keep an open mind. And, anyway, what about the hymn?"

"Hymn?"

"All things bright and beautiful, miss. *All* things, see? Which includes Spader's trunks, obviously."

"If they are Spader's trunks," said Nathan. "We don't actually know they are."

Miss Garden picked up her book and slammed it down on the desk again, hard. People jumped in their seats.

"I don't care whose they are," she breathed. "The next person who mentions trunks or anything to do with trunks, or even *looks* at them, will find himself – or herself – in detention. And I don't care if you think I'm overreacting. So be it."

She glared from face to face and the room fell silent. Peter Smith said not another word, but he did widen his eyes and turn his head slowly, and stare at the trunks.

"Peter!"

"I can't help it, miss. You get drawn to them."

"You'll get drawn to detention if you don't stop now."

His head snapped to the front, held there for a second, then wrenched back in the direction of the radiator, as if some huge hand had turned it like a tap. "That's it," Miss Garden said. "That's enough. Bring me your diary!"

Peter Smith heaved himself out of his desk and took his diary to the front, where the cover fell off and fluttered to the ground. Miss Garden waited, disdainfully, while he picked it up.

"You can't say you weren't warned," she said.

"Oh no, miss. Fair enough."

"Do you have any after-school commitments?" she asked, thumbing through the grubby book so she could write in the detention.

Peter Smith seemed not to hear. He shrugged and smiled round at the others, enjoying his time at the centre of the stage. When Miss Garden looked up, she found herself staring at the back of his head.

"You puzzle me, you know," she said quietly. "You don't look it, but you act like a complete fool."

"Hmm?" he said, turning back to her.

"Did you hear what I just said?"

"Sorry, miss. Yes, miss. Only on Wednesdays."

"A complete fool only on Wednesdays? Really?"

"No. I mean..."

"Because today is Tuesday and it seems to me you're behaving like an utter noodle today."

Exactly, thought Graham. A complete and utter noodle. Peter Smith, however, didn't seem to mind being called a noodle. He smiled and lowered his eyes modestly, as if he were thinking, "Me, miss? A noodle? How kind of you to say so."

At lunchtime Graham made his way to the sandwich room in one of the temporary huts. They were rickety grey buildings and had been temporary since about 1975, but Graham liked them. He nodded at Mr Trainor, who sat at the front plodding through a pile of exercise books, then dropped into the seat next to Nathan and started unpacking his lunch box.

"You're still with us, then," said Nathan, chewing slowly.

"What?"

"You haven't conked out or anything."

"How do you mean 'conked out'?"

"Swimming trunk fumes."

"Oh, that. No, I managed to overcome it."

"They're all noodles now, you know."

"Who are?"

Sometimes it was hard to work out what Nathan was talking about. He didn't always offer you enough words to make into proper sentences.

"Peter Smith and that lot," he said. "Angela Carr. George. They're all noodles now."

"What's new? They always were."

"No, I mean they've decided they like the idea. They were calling each other noodles all through German. 'You complete noodle.' 'You utter noodle.' Stuff like that."

Graham was arranging his lunch in little piles in front of him. He stopped and looked at Nathan.

"That's ridiculous," he said. "You can't be *proud* to be a noodle."

"They are."

"Ridiculous."

"I suppose so. Mind you, if you are a noodle, it sort of makes sense."

"How?"

"Well, you wouldn't *know* it's nothing to be proud of, would you?"

Graham snorted in agreement and picked up an egg sandwich.

"They're going to miss the boat, that lot," he said.

"What boat?"

"Miss the boat, Nathan. You know. Life. Spoil their chances."

"Miss the life-boat."

"In a manner of speaking, yes. After all, we're here to learn, aren't we? You can't spend your life arsing around. Your whole future's ahead of you. You have to think of that."

Which is what Graham's dad often said. Your future's ahead of you, Graham. Don't squander it.

"It always is, though, isn't it?" said Nathan.

"What?"

"Your future. It can't be behind you, can it?"

Graham suspended his sandwich halfway to his mouth.

"That's what I'm saying," he said. "You waste your youth being a noodle and that's how you end up. An adult noodle. And what use is that to anybody?"

"Very true."

"There's more interesting things to do in life. And to talk about."

They ate slowly and in silence for a while, staring at the Greek posters that had adorned the walls of the sandwich room for as long as anyone could remember. The notion that Peter Smith and his cronies actually liked being noodles irritated Graham. He couldn't quite say why, but it did.

After lunch they shook out the crumbs and wandered into the crisp air of Yard Two. Graham took with him a piece of his mum's seedcake in a paper bag. He always saved the seedcake till last, and more often than not took it outside to eat. Yard Two thronged with kids. Some chased balls. Some just chased. Others lounged around, leaning against walls, talking or playing cards with gloved hands. Graham noticed a little gathering by the music block. They looked to be neither chasers nor loungers, but stood, staring intently inwards like people at a funeral. He nudged Nathan and they ambled over to see what was going on.

They might have guessed.

A small space had been left clear at the centre of the group, and Peter Smith was standing in it. Cold as the day was, he had removed his school sweatshirt and knotted it over his head like a turban. He held himself perfectly still and straight, a dancer waiting for the music to start. His eyes were closed and on the ground at his feet was his brief-case. George Marriott stood nearby, one arm raised, looking at his watch.

"What's going on?" Graham asked.

The girl in front of him turned and shushed in his face.

"I only asked."

"Shush!"

Then George dropped his hand, and Peter Smith began to make a thin whining sound through his teeth. He flapped his arms and sprang over the brief-case.

"Bah-dom! Bah-dom!"

He lifted a knee, twisted round, and sprang back over the case.

"Bah-dom! Bah-dom!"

Graham looked briefly at Nathan, but he, like the others, was frowning with concentration and completely intent.

"Bah-domby-domby-dom-dom-DOM!"

Peter Smith leapt up and landed square on the brief-case. Graham was appalled.

"Good grief!" he said. "That's a perfectly good brief-case. He just jumped on a perfectly good brief-case."

"Shush," said Nathan.

George, meanwhile, had stepped into the ring and declared a foul.

"Foul? Why?" asked Smith.

"You got the words wrong."

"They're not words – they're sounds."

"You got the sounds wrong, then. It should go 'Domby-domby-dom-dom-DOM!'"

"That's what I did."

"No. You went, *Bah*-domby-domby-dom-dom-DOM!"

"What a pair of chuffers," Graham muttered, though not loud enough for anyone to hear.

Peter Smith was shaking his head and smiling.

"You're nit-picking, Marriott," he said, "and anyway you ought to know the rules don't count."

"Don't count?" said George, his voice rising to a squeak. "What have we got 'em for if they don't count?"

"A Noodle doesn't abide by rules. A Noodle is *against* rules. But we can use them when we *want* to."

"And when's that?"

"When's that, George? When's that? Only on Wednesdays, of course."

There were murmurs of approval from some of the onlookers. Graham snorted and immediately wished he hadn't. Peter Smith walked over to him.

"Ah," he said. "It's Graham Keefe. Are you a Noodle, Gray?"

"No, I am not."

"I thought not. And what have we here?"

With a dramatic lunge, Peter Smith grabbed the bag of seedcake.

"Oi! Give that back! My mum made that."

"Mrs Keefe's exceedingly good cake," said Peter Smith, his nose in the bag. "A piece of cake."

He studied it closely through one wide eye, then held it up for all to see.

"Oh dear," he said. "Oh dear, oh dear, oh dear. What a poor specimen of a cake. Every Noodle knows a cake should be good on the tongue *and* good on the eye. But this cake ... this cake may taste good but it looks like a floor tile."

Then he dropped it, leapt squawking into the air, and landed on it with both feet.

"Oi!"

The small crowd cheered.

"What do you think you're doing? That was my mum's cake!"

"It *was* your mum's cake, true, but it's better off as a floor tile. I think she'd agree, don't you?"

"You daft nelly," said Graham. "You've flattened a perfectly good piece of seedcake."

"You didn't want it, did you?"

"Of course I bloody wanted it!"

"But, Gray, Gray, don't look so disappointed. This is what a Noodle does. He points out things like this. He lives on a higher plane."

"By stamping on perfectly decent cake?"

"But of course."

Graham looked down at the cake and for a second he saw his mother biting her lip with concentration as she took it from the oven. He wanted to say something sharp and unpleasant to Smith but he was lost for words and far too humiliated. In the distance the bell sounded for the end of lunch and the crowd began to disperse, chatting and animated.

"I told you," Nathan said quietly as they streamed past. "They're really into this Noodle business now."

"They want sorting out," said Graham. "That's sick, that is. Treading on people's cake is sick."

Nathan squatted over the cake and poked it with a finger.

"I thought Smith liked cake," he said.

"He likes *fancy* cake. He's too precious to

appreciate honest-to-goodness, straightforward cake."

"Down-to-earth cake, you might say. Shall I scrape it up?"

"I'm not going to eat it now, am I, Nathan? Use your head."

"Sorry. I just thought..."

"Well, don't bother. Look at it. Just look at it. That was theft, that was."

"It can't be theft, Graham. It's still there, isn't it?"

"Then it's criminal damage. They're mad. They shouldn't get away with stuff like that."

And they won't, he thought suddenly. They won't get away with it.

He didn't know what he was going to do about it, but he was determined to pay them back for this. He waited for the others to reach the main doors before he moved. Then he turned abruptly and almost ploughed into a small round-faced girl who'd been standing just behind him.

"Whatcher," she said cheerily.

Graham blinked at her. He had no idea who she was. She smiled up at him from beneath a straight blonde fringe. He was perplexed.

"You're Keith, aren't you?" she said.

"What?"

"Keith."

"No," said Nathan from over his shoulder. "Keefe. Keefe, Graham."

"Keith Graham. Right. Shame about the cake."

"It's Graham Keefe, actually," said Graham shortly. "Anyway, what's it to you?"

"Right," said the girl. "I've got it now. And I'm Beth."

She beamed and began to move away.

"See you around, Keith," she called back at him.

He watched her trot off to catch up with the others.

"What was that about?" Nathan asked.

"Search me. I've never seen her before in my life."

"Weird."

Graham shook his head.

"No," he said. "She just muddled me up with someone else."

"All the same, it's weird," said Nathan. "Maybe she's a Noodle too."

Mr Legge appeared at the school doors and surveyed the yard. He was short and bullish with tight curly hair. He saw them standing mournfully by the patch of cake and bellowed at them to get a move on. As they trailed in, he clapped a friendly arm round Graham's shoulder.

"Graham," he said. "Not like you to be so tardy."

"No, sir. Someone trod on my cake, sir."

"Really?"

The eyes in Mr Legge's rugby-hardened face managed to show concern.

"Tell me about it," he said.

"It's all right, thanks, sir," said Graham. "I can handle it."

ANTI-NOODLES

Throughout the afternoon, Graham found it hard to concentrate.

"Criminal damage," he kept saying to himself. "He could end up inside if he goes on like that."

He was looking at a sheet of French conversation but all he could see were Smith's grinning face and the cake, flattened and yellow, with the crinkled imprint of a Noodle's shoe all over it. He tried to shake it out of his head, but the picture sneaked back. Sometimes the round face of the strange Beth girl was there too, peering out of the crowd and smiling. He wondered whether there was any genuine sympathy in that smile, or whether she was, like Smith, merely grinning.

Smith. Peter Smith. He'll end up inside. He *ought* to end up inside. Smith, the hardened criminal, banged up for destroying a banquet in the Town Hall.

"Why?" the judge asks. "This is a wanton and a thoughtless thing to do, and you are to receive the full penalty the law allows ... but *why*? Why did you do it?"

"It's an art form, Your Ludship," says a forty-year-old Smith. "The art of the Noodles!"

He makes a clenched fist and the judge recoils in horror.

"The Noodles! I might have known. Take him down!"

Graham tried to summon up Smith's cell in crisp detail but somehow the image wouldn't form properly. He didn't really know what the cells were like. His dad had signed the Official Secrets Act when he became a prison officer, and he took it seriously. He told Graham next to nothing about his work.

"I can't even tell you how many socks we have in there," he used to say, deliberately tightening his lips.

So all that Graham could picture now was his dad unlocking Smith's cheerfully decorated cell and taking him a mug of tea. It wasn't an entirely satisfying thought. His dad would probably smile at Smith and be matey – Graham could hardly remember him being angry – and someone being angry was what was needed now.

* * *

On the way home that afternoon, they almost ran into the Noodles again. There were three of them this time – Peter Smith, George Marriott and Angela Carr – and they were loitering outside the cinema. As soon as he caught sight of them, Graham dug his elbow in Nathan's side and moved his eyebrows up and down.

"What?"

"It's them," said Graham. "Just by the Complex."

"Who?"

"Don't get too close. People might think we're with them."

"What are they up to now?" Nathan asked, sounding rather too interested, Graham thought.

They were hopping along by the glass front of the cinema. In single file. Peter Smith had a bag of crisps and, from time to time, he stopped and attempted to feed some to a lamp-post.

"Completely out of their skulls," Graham said.

A woman in fancy glasses was peering at them through the doors of the Complex. After a while she came out and stood in front of them, her arms folded. She had a ball of wool and two needles in one hand. Peter Smith offered her a crisp.

"Don't you think it's sad?" he asked the

woman. "These lampposts are so *thin*. Unless we can fatten them up, people are going to walk right into them."

The woman looked from the Noodles to the lamppost and back.

"Clear off," she said. "We've got a queue forming here in a minute."

"Ooh, a queue," said George. "Can we be in it?"

"No. Shove off. You're causing a disturbance."

She brandished the knitting needles at them, like someone trying to ward off vampires, and watched them hop off down the street. When Graham and Nathan reached the woman, she was standing with her hands on her hips, staring after them.

"It's a phase they're going through," Graham told her confidentially. "They call themselves Noodles."

The woman gave a jump and backed away a little.

"Clear off out of it," she said.

"No," said Graham. "We're not Noodles. The opposite, in fact..."

"Listen, I know your school. If you don't clear off right now, I'm going straight in to phone it up. Bunch of nutters."

"You don't understand..."

"Right now!" said the woman, taking a step towards them.

Nathan took Graham by the elbow and pulled him away.

"Leave it," he said. "It's too tricky to explain."

"But she thinks we're Noodles."

"Let her, Graham. It really doesn't matter."

"Of course it matters. I'm not having people think I'm a Noodle."

But Nathan was dragging him across the street.

"Listen," he said with uncharacteristic force, "you want to do something about the Noodles, then get on and do it. Don't waste your time arguing with strangers."

"Do what?"

"I don't know. They've made themselves into a group. Maybe you should do the same."

"Another branch of the Noodles? Don't be daft."

"Well then, something that stands for what the Noodles *don't*. The Anti-Noodles or something."

The idea stopped Graham in his tracks.

"The Anti-Noodles," he mused.

"Well, I don't know. Maybe not..."

"No, no. You've hit the nail on the head, Nathan."

"Have I? That makes a change."

"Yes. Brilliant. The Anti-Noodles. That's what we'll be from now on."

"We? This is your battle, not mine."

"Oh, come on, Nathan. You don't want that lot running around unchecked, do you?"

"It doesn't bother me really..."

"Of course it bothers you. So that's what we are, you and me. The Anti-Noodles."

Graham dummied a punch at his friend and looked cheerful for the first time that day. Nathan nodded and gave him a thin smile.

"All right," he said ponderously. "If you like."

Then he saw something over Graham's shoulder and his eyes widened.

"Look, look," he breathed. "Behind you. Over there."

Graham turned and looked. The woman from the cinema was still standing on guard, glowering at them through her flashing glasses and moving her mouth as if she were grumbling under her breath.

"Not her," said Nathan. "Over there."

He gave a short stabbing point but Graham still didn't understand. All he could see, threading her way through the shoppers, was a girl from the Sixth Form College. He could tell she was from the Sixth Form College by the way she walked, coolly and confidently, with a rucksack slung over her shoulder. Graham didn't know her.

"So?" he said.

"Look, look," repeated Nathan through clenched teeth.

She had dark hair piled up on her head with a wisp hanging down by each ear, and she had large eyes. Even at this distance Graham could see she had large, rather stunning eyes. Then he saw, trotting along beside her, a little round figure, jabbering intently and putting in the odd skip to keep up. This one Graham did know. He looked round for a shop door to hide in, but it was too late.

"Oh! Look at this. It's Keith again!"

She stopped and beamed at them. The other girl stopped too, but showed no sign of smiling.

"This is the one I was just telling you about," said Beth. "The one with the cake."

And this time there was a flicker of a smile from the dark-haired girl.

"It's Graham, actually," said Nathan.

"No, not you. Him. Keith. Funny, we was just talking about you, Keith..."

"No. I'm Nathan and this is Graham."

"Oh, yes. That's right. I'll get it next time. I was telling Amanda about the cake getting squashed and stuff, you know. This is Amanda. Amanda Rayburn. She's my sister. My big sister," she added unnecessarily. "It's funny really because I was just saying about your dad when suddenly there you are."

"My dad?"

"Yes."

Why? Why were they talking about his dad?

Graham narrowed his eyes and looked from Beth to her sister. Amanda brushed a strand of dark hair coolly from her cheek and heaved a sigh, deliberately loud. My sister bores me, it seemed to say, and so do you two. She grabbed Beth by her collar.

"Come on," she said. "We've got to go."

Then she headed briskly into the supermarket. Beth followed, dancing along sideways.

"Bye, Keith," she called. "Bye, Keith's friend."

The supermarket doors swished shut and they were gone.

"Are you sure you don't know her?" Nathan asked.

"Of course I don't."

"Or her sister?"

"No."

"Then what was that about your dad?"

"Search me."

"Maybe it's to do with ... you know."

"What?"

"What he does. Up at the prison."

Maybe it was. The fact that his dad was a prison officer gave Graham some notoriety around the school. Some people didn't like the idea, and said so, but others found it rather glamorous and pumped him for details. Of course, he couldn't give them any. He would've liked to, but the Official Secrets Act always got in the way. He glanced at the supermarket window and saw Beth and her sister swinging down an aisle with a basket.

"Come on," he said. "If we don't get moving they'll be out again. Let's merge."

They set off in the direction of the roundabout, merging with the crowds as they went. Merging was a ploy they adopted from time to time. It involved moving rather like clockwork and staring with their mouths half-open.

"Do you think we should recruit?" Graham asked after a while.

"Recruit?"

"More people. To be Anti-Noodles."

"If you like. They'd probably need to know what we'd plan to do, though."

Graham wondered about that. What would they do? Somehow, the *idea* of the Anti-Noodles was clearer than the fact.

"There'll be plenty to do," he said vaguely.

"Like what?"

"Well ... we'll be *against* the Noodles, won't we?"

"That's not actually doing anything, though. I mean, I'm against Physics, but I don't join an Anti-Physics Society, do I?"

"Maybe you should."

"Maybe. But I'd still want to know what an Anti-Physics Society would do."

"You've strayed off the point, Nathan. The Noodles aren't a subject, they're a movement. It's like politics. You have a government and you have an opposition, and the whole point of the opposition is to be anti the government."

"Yes," said Nathan thoughtfully. "Though I'm not really sure about that either. It all seems a bit pointless."

"OK, OK, we'll do something practical. Like get them back for what they did to my cake."

"Why don't you just forget about the cake, Graham? It's getting to you, I can tell, and it's not really that important."

"Easy for you to say when it wasn't your cake. Look, I suggest we both give the matter some thought and compare notes tomorrow morning. Right?"

"Right," said Nathan, trying to sound enthusiastic.

When they met at the school gates on the following morning, Graham gave Nathan a greeting nod and asked him if he'd come up with anything.

"Nothing much," said Nathan.

"Nothing? What, *absolutely* nothing?"

"Every time I thought about it I kind of lost the point."

"What do you mean by that?"

"I couldn't quite remember what the Anti-Noodles actually were."

"They're us."

"I know that, but *why*?"

Just then someone elbowed between them and shot off through the gates. It was George Marriott. They stopped to watch him. He was going at such a rate that he banked as he rounded the corner by the caretaker's cottage. Which was unusual. George's normal progress was a sort of loose slouch. And he'd smartened himself up. He was so smart that they didn't recognize him at first.

"That is why we're Anti-Noodles," said Graham. "Look at him."

George, stiff-legged and swinging his arms, pointed his way through the crowd with a rolled umbrella. He looked like those business types who steam up and down the streets of the City, almost but not quite running. He could've been set down in the middle of London, Graham thought, and not been out of place. Except for his tie which he wore on his forehead so that it hung down between his eyes.

"What's the betting that Smith will turn up looking like that too?" said Graham.

"Short odds, I should think."

They were right. They encountered Peter Smith five minutes later in one of the lower corridors. His tie was also neatly suspended from his forehead and he gave them a friendly wave with his umbrella.

"Morning, gents," he said. "Business as

usual, I trust."

Graham scowled and didn't answer.

At lunch Graham met Nathan in the sandwich room to compare notes and make plans.

"I spotted about half a dozen," Nathan said. "All with ties and umbrellas."

"Pillocks," huffed Graham.

"So what are we going to do about it?"

"We have to show them up for what they really are."

"Pillocks?"

"Exactly."

"How?"

"Why do you always ask the questions?" said Graham. "Why can't you come up with a few answers?"

"Because I'm not a very original person. It said so in my report."

"I know what you can do," chipped in a squeaky voice several places behind them.

Graham twisted round to look, but he already knew who it was.

"What are you doing here?" he said.

"Eating sandwiches," said Beth.

"Since when did you have sandwiches? I've never seen you in here before."

"I just started today," she beamed at him. "Mum said it was a good idea. She said it was cheaper and..."

"It was her idea, was it?"

"No, it was my idea because..."

"I thought it might've been, somehow. This is a private conversation, you know."

"I know, Keith. About the Noodles."

"For the last time it is not Keith, it is Graham. Graham Keefe."

"How do you do, Graham?"

Nathan stopped chewing, put down his sandwich and looked at her for a second or two.

"What *can* we do?" he said.

"Don't ask," said Graham. "It's none of her business."

"But if she's got an idea..."

"I have."

"An idea, Nathan? You think she's got an idea? Just look at her."

Nathan looked. She was nibbling crisps and smiling broadly at them.

"I see what you mean," he said.

"I have got an idea," said Beth. "If you let me join, I'll tell you what it is."

"No thanks."

"Maybe I'll tell you anyway."

"Don't bother."

Nathan picked up his sandwich again.

"No harm in asking, though, is there?" he said. "After all, the Anti-Noodles is supposed to be a *group*. How can it be a group if there's just the two of us?"

"He's got a point there, Graham," said Beth.

"All right, *ask* her. Then see if I'm right."

Graham extended his hand in mock politeness at Beth.

"Pray, do reveal your brilliant notion," he said.

She got up, wiped her hands on her skirt, and moved to the table directly behind them. Then she folded her arms and leaned forward.

"Send 'em on a message," she said in a low voice, looking from Graham to Nathan with sparkling eyes.

"Send 'em on a message? What's that supposed to mean?"

"It's what someone done at my last school. Sent this boy called ... now, what *was* he called? Tim or Tom or something like that."

"Tony?" suggested Nathan.

"I don't think so. He had flappy ears and he was a bit of a bully..."

"It doesn't matter what he was called," said Graham. "What did he do?"

"Well," said Beth, leaning further forward, "he went to the staffroom with this message. 'Mr Hollioake would like to borrow the elbow grease for a moment.' I think it was Mr Hollioake. Anyway, the thing is – in case you don't know – there isn't any such thing as elbow grease. It's a kind of made-up thing. Only this boy with the ears – Tim, or Tom it might've been – didn't know that."

"Hey, that's not bad," said Nathan with a

nod of approval. "What happened then?"

"He made a right nelly of himself, that's what happened. And that's what I think we should do with the Noodles. Make 'em look like nellies."

"They'd never fall for it," said Graham.

"Not for elbow grease," said Nathan, "but they might fall for something else."

"Possibly."

"Course they would," said Beth brightly. "So. Can I join?"

Graham concentrated on unwrapping a slice of malt loaf.

"Well?"

"We'll think about it," said Nathan.

"Go on. I just helped you out, didn't I?"

"You're a bit pushy, aren't you?" said Graham. "All this 'Hello, Keith, how are you?' As if you know me."

"I do know you."

"You don't know me."

"I sort of do. From what the other kids have said."

"And what's that?"

"About what your dad does. I thought that was interesting. I like to take an interest in interesting things. You know, like what people's parents do."

For a brief moment she looked serious. Then she turned to Nathan.

"What does yours do?" she asked.

"My dad? Nothing. I mean, I haven't got one."

"Why not?"

"He ran off with a woman from work."

"Ran off! Wow! Where'd he go?"

"To Nottingham."

"Wow! All the way to Nottingham! What's she like? Have you seen her?"

"Well," said Nathan, putting down his sandwich again, "she's all right, I suppose, but..."

"Don't tell her," Graham said indignantly. "Nosey little baggage."

"No I'm not. I'm just being chatty."

"Asking about people's dads' other women is not being chatty. It's downright rude. How would you like it?"

"My dad hasn't got another woman. He's got Mum. But he doesn't live with us either. So I'm the same as what's-'is-name here."

"Nathan."

"That's right. The same as you. So there's just me and Trish – that's my mum – and Amanda. Amanda's my sister. You saw her yesterday by the shops. She's good-looking, isn't she?"

"Yes," said Nathan. "Very nice."

"I might look like that when I'm older. Except for the hair colour."

"I doubt it," said Graham flatly.

"So where's your dad, then?" asked Nathan.

"In Africa."

"Africa?"

"He's out there working on a dam. It's very important work, actually. He sends us these fantastic postcards about gorillas and stuff. They get a lot of grief from gorillas. The gorillas come into the camp and bend all the aerials and pinch the grub. What about you?" she added to Graham without taking a breath.

"What?"

"Your dad."

"No. He's never been known to bend an aerial in his life."

"No, I mean working in a prison. It must be interesting."

"He can't tell you," explained Nathan. "He's signed the Official Secrets Act."

"Graham's signed the Official Secrets Act?"

"No. His dad's signed. So he can't say. So Graham doesn't know much."

"Wow! Like spies and things."

"Not very like, no," said Graham, wrapping up the rest of his sandwiches and stuffing them in his bag. "I've got to go. See you around."

He stood abruptly and strode outside where he took a deep breath of cool air.

"Pushy little maggot," he said to himself.

Nathan clattered down the wooden steps behind him.

"What's the hurry?" he asked. "You could get an ulcer charging about like that after eating."

"I could get an ulcer listening to her talk."

"She's all right. A bit potty, that's all."

"Hmm."

"Interesting what she said, though. About the message idea, I mean. I reckon that might work, don't you?"

Graham pretended he hadn't heard.

PIGS

Their plans were ready by the middle of the following week. Graham found Peter Smith during the afternoon break. He was standing motionless in the middle of Yard Two with his hands on his hips and his mouth open.

"It's living art," Nathan explained. "There's two or three of them dotted around the place. Just standing there, like statues."

"It may be art," said Graham, "but it's not what I'd call living."

He went up to Smith and tapped him on the shoulder.

"Can't talk," said Smith. "I'm an exhibit."

"I've got a message for you, though. From Miss Garden."

"Ah," said Smith, turning round. "Tomorrow's detention."

"No..."

"She's released me from captivity. I knew

she would."

Smith's eyes peered at him from either side of his tie. It was a bit disconcerting but Graham was determined not to give him the satisfaction of a reaction.

"Not exactly," he said coolly. "She's got a job for you."

"I don't normally do jobs. Only on Wednesdays."

"This is Wednesday."

"Then she's in luck. What's the mission? Something impossible, I trust?"

"It's not impossible," said Graham, "but it sounds a bit daft."

"A bit daft! Oh, super. Soo-per. She knew who to come to, then. Deliver the message, Bloodaxe."

For some inexplicable reason, Smith had taken to calling Graham Bloodaxe. The name niggled him but, again, he refused to react.

"She says would you go to the kitchens and collect a sack of scraps."

"What for?"

"Leftover food. To take to the staffroom for Mr Legge."

"Leggy wants a sack of leftovers? He must be desperate."

"It's not for him. It's for the school pig."

"What, Spader?"

"No, a real pig. *The* pig, you know."

"No."

"Oh, haven't you heard? They're putting a pig in the copse at the back of the top field."

"This makes no sense, Bloodaxe. They sell raffle tickets to buy a minibus and instead they buy a pig. You can't take a football team to away matches on a pig. Have they thought of that?"

"I think it's to study, actually," said Graham, "but it doesn't make a lot of sense, I agree."

This was the beauty of the idea. The notion of a school pig seemed so unlikely that it rang true. And Graham could pretend to be bemused. A pig? Don't ask me why they want a pig.

"Don't ask me why they want a pig," he said. "I can think of better things to study. But apparently they want to do a GCSE in Animal Husbandry so..."

"There's more puzzlement in this than meets the eye, though," interrupted Smith. "Why ask you to ask me to ask the kitchens for scraps? It's a bit round the houses, isn't it? A pig could starve while all that was going on."

"It hasn't turned up yet..."

"But why me?"

Graham hadn't thought of that. He mumbled something about doing pig duty instead of detention.

"Not to worry, Bloodaxe," said Smith. "I'm

intrigued by this. I *want* to go. In fact, this is Noodle business *par excellence*. Stand aside. I'm about to go foraging."

And off he went. Graham looked round and saw Nathan emerging from behind the caretaker's hedge. He gave him a thumbs-up sign.

They positioned themselves in the bay outside the staffroom and pretended to be engrossed in the noticeboard. After three or four minutes, they heard a scraping sound and Peter Smith came struggling backwards down the corridor, dragging behind him a large black plastic sack. He stopped by the door, straightened up and knocked. A young teacher they'd never seen before came to the door, gaped at Smith and, after a hushed exchange, disappeared back into the staffroom. Then Mr Legge came to the door. He had a mug in his hand and a puzzled expression on his face.

"What's all this?" he said sharply.

"It's your leftovers, sir."

Smith undid the top of the sack and invited Mr Legge to take a closer look. Mr Legge bent over the sack and almost immediately arched back, his face twisted with disgust. He recoiled against the door, slopping coffee everywhere.

"What the devil are you playing at, Smith?" he said.

"It's for the pig, sir."

"You said it was for me."

"Yes, sir, it is but..."

"Are you suggesting..."

"No, no, sir, of course not."

"And take that stupid tie off!" Mr Legge shouted, suddenly. "How do you expect me to talk to someone with a tie hanging all over their face?"

Smith tried to wrench the tie off but only managed to twist it to one side and tighten the knot.

"Sorry, sir," he said. "It's stuck."

Mr Legge folded his arms and looked at him severely for a moment or two.

"Let's start again," he said quietly. "This is for me, is it?"

"Yes, sir. Well, for the pig..."

"There you go again!"

Smith blinked and stiffened.

"Tarting around with stupid ties is one thing, Smith. Insulting members of staff another thing entirely."

"Yes, sir."

"Get rid of this garbage and then come straight back here with your diary. Do you understand?"

"Yes, sir."

"Then go!"

The staffroom door slammed and Peter Smith heaved a huge sigh. When he saw Graham and Nathan ambling over to him, he narrowed his eyes and a kind of understanding dawned on his face.

"You did this," he said, breathing hard. "You set me up."

"Indeed we did," said Graham with a sweet smile. "A little offering, courtesy of the Anti-Noodles."

"The what?"

"The Anti-Noodles. Shouldn't be too difficult to work out, Peter. You're the Noodles, we're the Anti-Noodles."

Smith's mouth flapped open, but soundlessly.

"You want a hand with the sack?" asked Nathan.

"I expect he does," said Graham. "Sad, really. Because we don't do sacks. Not today, anyway. Never on Wednesdays. See you around, Smith."

Graham's group grew in size. They weren't as plentiful as the Noodles – there were only three of them – but anyone could join the Noodles: they weren't fussy. The Anti-Noodles were more particular. Their third member wasn't Beth, however.

"We're thinking about it," Graham had told her after she'd pleaded to be admitted for the fifth or sixth time.

"But, Graham, I'm useful and handy..."

"Look, we're having a meeting at the weekend. We'll talk about it, OK?"

"OK, Graham."

And she'd gone tripping off, humming to herself. Which unsettled Graham. Why couldn't she see that they didn't want her? He tried to let her down lightly, but she kept coming back, like a dog with a stick.

"She probably is quite handy, though," Nathan suggested.

"How do you work that out?"

"What with her dad building dams in Africa."

"Ah, well," said Graham darkly. "That's another thing. Africa. And gorillas."

"What about them?"

"I was thinking about the school pig. I mean, if we had a school pig, it probably *would* eat leftovers. That would be natural for a pig. But a gorilla – well, they're different. I looked them up. They're like Jo Crisp."

"Who?"

"That tall girl in Year Eight."

"Like a gorilla?"

"Yes. Well, not to look at, no, but she's what you might call a naturally shy vegetarian, and gorillas are too. They're sort of gentle and they slouch about picking at stalks with these leathery hands. What they don't do is get together and raid human camps. 'OK, you guys, let's bomb over to the dam-builders and bend a few aerials. Maybe we could pick up some pizzas while we're there...' No, it's all a little bit fishy, if you ask me."

And he tapped the side of his nose knowingly. So Beth wasn't their third recruit. Vicki Kember was.

Nathan suggested her.

"Why her?" Graham asked.

"She's sensible."

"Yes."

"And ... well..."

"What?"

"She's got neat handwriting."

"True. I don't see how that's going to help, though."

"You never know, Graham. It might be *very* helpful one day."

"No other reason, then?"

"No, not especially," said Nathan and blushed. "Just, you know, the sensibleness. And the handwriting."

Graham liked to do things properly so he wrote the names of the Anti-Noodles in a book. The key to a successful group, he considered, was organization. That's what Dad always said. Organize, Graham. It'll save you a lot of trouble in the long run.

They held their first official meeting in Graham's shed on Saturday afternoon. The first half hour was given over to a re-run of the Pigswill Caper. Nathan and Graham told Vicki the story in careful detail and then watched silently as Vicki wrote a brief account in the book.

"Have you put in the bit about Leggy slopping his coffee all over the place?" Nathan said.

"No."

"We ought to put that in. It was a classic moment."

"I can't put everything in," Vicki said without looking up from the book. "It's not very efficient."

"Why not?"

"Because if you think about it, the whole incident took about five minutes, but to write down everything would take about two hours. It's out of proportion."

"Good thinking, Vic," Graham said.

When she'd finished they went on to the next item on the agenda: what to do next. Vicki said the Pigswill Caper was very good as far as it went, but perhaps it was a bit negative. Couldn't they do something that was ... well, some *use* to people?

"I mean, we don't just want to wait for the Noodles to do something ridiculous and then do something ridiculous back," she said.

"You're not suggesting the Pigswill Caper was ridiculous, I hope," Graham said.

"Of course not, but it wasn't actually *useful*, was it?"

"Depends how you look at it."

"No, forget the Noodles for a while," Vicki said. "This –" she delved into her bag "– is nothing to do with the Noodles."

She brought out a letter which she unfolded and put on an old flower pot so the others could see. Graham caught sight of the school address and the word confidential.

"I've had this letter from Mr Campbell Barker," Vicki went on. "Actually, no one must know about it, but I reckon it's all right to tell you two."

"Thanks very much."

"It's about Mr Legge," she said, and then, making the words with her lips but no sound, she added, "He's leaving."

"What?" breathed Nathan.

"It's Mr Legge. He's leaving."

"Why are we whispering?" Graham said.

"Because it's confidential."

They followed the direction of her glance at the door and could almost imagine a crowd gathered outside with their ears cocked.

"Old Leggy's leaving?" said Nathan. "I didn't know that."

"Of course not. Nobody knows. Yet."

"So how come you do?" Graham asked.

"Well, they're having a do for him – a kind of farewell dinner – and CB wants me to write out the place names."

"Place names?"

"Yes. The names of all the guests on bits of

card. So they know where to sit."

"And what's this got to do with us?"

"This is what I'm saying. Maybe it's something the Anti-Noodles could do as a group."

"Why?"

She gave a short, deliberate sigh.

"Because it's useful. Helpful. We can say we had a hand in it. I mean, Robin Hood didn't just sit around in the forest pigging himself on venison, did he? He robbed the rich to give to the poor."

"Robin Hood?" said Nathan. "How does he come into it?"

"Don't you listen? By being helpful, you clot!"

"All right, all right," Graham said. "Keep your voice down."

"Well, what do you think?" Vicki asked. "Are we going to try to do something useful or not?"

Nathan stroked his chin and looked thoughtful.

"Hmm," he said. "I suppose it might just bring us some kudo."

Vicki gave him a pitying look.

"Kudos," she said.

"Yes," Nathan said, blushing. "Quite. I mean, we'd sort of get a name for helping out..."

"Which is the opposite of what the Noodles do," Graham added. "Yes, I like it."

Vicki brought out pens and card. She explained that Campbell Barker wanted the place names done in a special way. He'd made a little cut-out in the shape of a leg and drawn toes and a knee-cap on it.

"What we have to do," she said, "is write the first name on the calf and the surname on the thigh."

"Why?" said Nathan.

"Because his name," Vicki explained slowly, "is Legge."

"And what names do we have to put?" Graham asked.

"You two don't put any," said Vicki. "They want to be able to read them. I'll write the names and you can cut out the legs. He's sent me a list of names."

Graham took the list and let in unroll. It spooled almost to the floor.

"Crikey," he said. "There's hundreds."

"About eighty, actually. But there would be: Old Leggy's been at that school for centuries. Right, let's get organized. You cut out the legs, Nathan, and Graham can mark on the toes and things..."

"Do we have different legs for men and women?" Nathan asked.

"Of course not. Legs are the same for both, more or less."

"They're not," Graham said. "Women's legs are more shapely."

"Well, if you're going to be sexist about it..."

"That's not being sexist. It's a fact. And anyway, men's legs are more hairy."

"We could put a few felt-tip hairs on, I suppose," Nathan said.

"And how are they going to read their names with hair all over them?"

"OK then," Nathan said with a shrug. "The same legs for both. Both bare."

They set to work and for a while no one spoke. Then Graham asked, "I don't suppose he knows it's us, does he? Campbell Barker, I mean."

"He knows it's me, of course," said Vicki, "but he doesn't know about the Anti-Noodles. Not many people do."

"Then perhaps she should put a note in with the cards when we hand them in. Courtesy of the Anti-Noodles."

"If you like," Vicki said, "but you might have to explain what that means..."

She stopped and looked from Nathan to the piece of card he'd just handed her.

"What's this supposed to be?"

"What?"

"These balloons."

"They're not balloons," said Nathan. "They're toes."

"Well, they look like balloons to me. Can't you concentrate? CB's not going to accept these."

"Sorry," said Nathan.

It was easier to draw on toes and knees than it was to cut out legs, and easier to cut out legs than write in names, and soon the legs began to pile up at Vicki's elbow.

"What we really need," she said, "is another person to read out the names so I don't have to keep checking against the list."

And at that very moment, there was a timid tap on the shed door. They froze and looked at each other. Vicki shoved the name-list back in her bag.

"Who is it?" Graham asked.

"Me," came a tiny voice.

It was Toby, Graham's little brother. Graham breathed a sigh of relief.

"Shove off, Tobe," he said. "This is grown-up stuff. You'll get in the way."

"I got something for yer."

"What?"

"Something out here."

"Well, obviously. What is it?"

"Open up and I'll show yer."

Graham huffed with annoyance and tugged open the door. Toby was standing there looking fed up. The top half of a smiling round face was peering over his shoulder. They couldn't actually see the smile but they knew it was there somewhere.

"Whatcher," said Beth.

"What's she doing here?"

"She come to the door. Then she come straight in. I couldn't get rid of her."

"This is a private meeting," Graham told Beth. "We're busy."

"I thought you might be. Have you decided yet? About me?"

"I had me cars all over the carpet," Toby moaned, "and she walked right through 'em."

Then he turned and stalked back to the house, leaving Beth grinning at the Anti-Noodles with her hands behind her back.

"Well?" she said. "Am I interrupting anything? Can I come in?"

"Yes," said Nathan and in she walked.

"What did you say that for?" Graham asked.

"I meant yes she is interrupting something," Nathan said. "She only heard the bit she wanted."

"This is nice," Beth said, smiling round at the flowerpots and garden tools. "Sort of cosy."

She put her head out of the door and surveyed the bottom of the garden.

"It's raggedy down this end, though, isn't it, Graham? Don't you ever do weeding and stuff?"

"Not down here, no," he answered grudgingly.

"His dad does the gardening," Nathan explained. "He says he only has time for a garden three-quarters the size of this one, so he leaves this bit wild."

"That's clever. What's the other side of that fence?"

"The road. You know, Hartley Road."

"Wow."

"Wow?" said Graham. "What's so wow about Hartley Road?"

She closed the door softly and lowered her voice.

"That's where the prison is. Jason told me. He's in my form. He's got a brother in the navy. Can you actually see the prison over your fence?"

"If you stand on a box. Look, we're holding a meeting here, not giving guided tours."

"I know, I know. Have you discussed about me joining? You said you would and I thought I'd come round..."

"We've had more important things to do than talk about you," Graham said. "Do you mind leaving us in peace?"

"Don't send her off," said Vicki. "She can read out the names for me. It's a bit of luck she turned up when she did."

"A bit of bad luck," Graham snapped, then turned on Beth. "Listen, you can't just call round people's houses."

"Why not? There's no harm in it. Anyway, the kid let me in, so I've been invited, haven't I?"

"Take no notice," Vicki told her. "He doesn't really mind."

"I do, I do."

Vicki ignored him and gave Beth the list of names.

"I've got this far," she said, pointing. "And I've got the rest to do. So if you just read them out..."

Beth picked up one of the cut-out legs and studied it.

"What's it in aid of?" she asked.

"There you are," Graham said. "Questions. If she helps, she's got to know what we're doing. And you said it was confidential."

"You won't tell anyone what we're doing, will you, Beth?"

"I don't know what you're doing."

"We have to cut out and label some cardboard legs, like these..."

"Cardboard legs," Beth said with a nod, as if it all made perfect sense. "Right-oh."

"Just don't think this means you're an Anti-Noodle," Graham muttered, snipping viciously at the next leg.

"Oh, don't be so miserable, Graham," said Vicki. "She can join if she wants. Why not?"

"Because she's a pain in the—"

"Nonsense. She just wants to be helpful, that's all. And, after all, that's what we're about."

"That's true," said Nathan slowly.

Graham darted him a glance which Nathan didn't notice, so busy was he trying to keep the next set of toes down to a reasonable size.

"It is what we agreed, isn't it, Graham?" Vicki said.

Graham shrugged and didn't answer. Being bossy sometimes went with being neat, it seemed. Maybe asking Vicki to join them hadn't been such a good idea. He preferred it when the Anti-Noodles were a bit more exclusive: just him and Nathan. Though even Nathan could be disappointing sometimes.

Maybe, he thought, I'm the only true Anti-Noodle there is.

They worked on and for a while only the sound of Beth reading out the names on the list punctuated the silence. Once or twice she paused and repeated a name which appealed to her.

"Harrington Regis. Actually, I wouldn't mind a name like that. People would take notice of you if you were called Harrington Regis."

"Not if you looked like Beth Rayburn," Graham said, half to himself.

Then Beth blinked at the list and said, "Bum."

"What was that?" Graham asked.

"Bum."

"Look, it's bad enough you coming round here uninvited without polluting the air with language..."

"And in one so young," said Nathan.

"No, Graham, I wasn't polluting the air. I was reading the list. It's one of the names."

"Bum?"

"With a double *M*. Bumm."

"Show me," said Vicki.

"German, probably," suggested Nathan.

"It's an odd name, though, isn't it?" said Beth. "Bumm?"

"All right, there's no need to keep saying it. This is my shed, you know."

Vicki took the list and found the place.

"Bumm," she said. "She's right. Basil Bumm."

She ran her finger a little further down the list.

"And look at this one. Dirk Lipp-Shudder. And this. Clytemnestra Pills..."

"He knows a funny lot of people, Old Leggy does," said Nathan.

"What do you mean, a funny lot of people?" Graham said, jumping to his feet. "These aren't real people. They can't be. This is all made up!"

For a second or two Graham felt like one of those cartoon characters walking across air with a bridge suddenly folded up under them. You're going to fall – you know you're going to fall – but there's a brief moment when you're suspended in midair. He grabbed the list and stared wildly at it.

"Warren Peace," he read. "Anna Bollick-Sterroid. Corin Nation..."

"Hmm," said Nathan, "I see what you mean."

"When did Campbell Barker give you this?" Graham asked, shaking the list at Vicki.

"Well..."

"Yes?"

"Now I come to think of it, he didn't actually *give* it to me. He left it on my desk at lunch."

"Exactly!" Graham said. "It's bloody Smith!"

"There's nothing wrong with that," Beth put in. "Smith's quite a normal sort of name. Bloody's a bit unusual, I suppose, but..."

"No, no," Graham barked at her. "Don't you see? We've been Noodled!"

They sat for a while staring at the floor, unsure of what to do or say.

"I'm sorry," Vicki said eventually in a quiet voice. "I just never imagined..."

"Don't worry about it," Nathan said. "Actually it was a clever move for a Noodle. Anyone would've been taken in."

"Really?" Graham said. "Would they?"

"Well, you were. You've just spent about an hour cutting out cardboard legs. You were taken in."

"Only because I listened to Vicki. Anyway, he must never know. Smith must never have the satisfaction of knowing that his little scheme worked."

"Then the thing to do now," said Beth, "is to burn 'em."

"Yes. Good. Burn them and then we can tell Smith his little ruse failed. 'Nice try, Noodle, but we were on to it.'"

"He'll know," said Nathan. "He'll just know it worked."

"Not if we keep our cool."

"He might know even then, actually," Vicki said.

"How?"

"Because he saw me collecting the card from the art store."

"Oh, great."

"He doesn't know what you wanted it for, though, does he?" said Beth. "You could pretend it was for something else."

"Look," Graham said, "do you have to keep chipping in? We were getting on all right till you turned up. Uninvited."

"Don't take it out on her, Graham," Vicki said. "It was my fault really."

"I just think she's bad news, that's all."

"I'm not bad news, Graham. I'm good news. You'll be glad I joined one day."

"What do you mean? You haven't joined."

"I have. Vicki said I have. What's wrong

with me, anyway?"

"Where shall I begin? For a start, you're not *serious* enough to be an Anti-Noodle..."

"I am. I'm deadly serious, Graham."

"You talk a load of rubbish..."

"No I don't."

"Oh no? What about all that stuff about delinquent gorillas swooping down on your dad's food supplies? What about that?"

"What's wrong with that?"

"Leave it alone, Graham," Nathan said.

"She asked what was wrong with her and I'm telling her. Gorillas don't do that kind of thing, Beth..."

"These ones did."

"I don't believe it."

She became rigid, her fists clenched by her side and her mouth suddenly turned down.

"You calling me a liar, are you?" she asked.

Graham didn't answer but raised his eyebrows. Then Beth walked out of the shed and slammed the door.

"What did you do that for?" Vicki asked.

"Do what? I didn't do anything."

"You did a bit," said Nathan. "You said she was a liar."

"I didn't actually say it. Anyway, she is."

"She's just a bit fanciful, that's all."

"But I told you. Gorillas don't do that. They really don't."

"Then maybe they weren't gorillas," Vicki

said sharply. "Maybe they were baboons or something. Anyway, what does it matter? You just took it out on her because you're miffed about being caught out by the Noodles. Don't you realize? The poor kid's lonely. She's only trying to be friendly."

"Well, she can be friendly somewhere else."

"We can all do that, Graham. We don't have to sit around in a mucky old shed being bossed about!"

Then she slammed out.

"Well," Graham said, turning to Nathan. "They're very touchy all of a sudden."

"She's got a point, though, Graham. Beth wasn't really doing any harm."

"Oh blast. Blast, blast, blast. I suppose I've got to creep round and apologize now."

Graham was expecting Nathan to say there'd be no need for that; that it would all blow over and be forgotten. But he didn't.

"It might help, actually," he said.

"Yes, well, I'll think about it," Graham said.

Then he slapped his knees and stood up.

"Come on," he said. "Let's burn these blasted legs."

SET MOVES

On Monday morning Graham was still feeling grouchy. He knew he'd have to seek Beth out and tell her he was sorry and he wasn't relishing the prospect. The sight of Peter Smith smirking at them as they approached the school gates didn't help.

"Busy weekend?" grinned Smith.

"Not particularly," Graham said. "Thanks for asking."

"No. I'm sure. Heard about Old Leggy leaving, did you?"

"We heard something about it, yes," said Nathan, and Graham gave him a sharp sideways glare.

"Thought you might have," said Smith. "Only it's not true apparently. Funny how these things get round, isn't it?"

"Highly amusing," said Graham.

"See you around, then," Smith said, and

went off, with an even wider smirk.

"Well, that was brilliant," Graham said to Nathan. "Now he *knows* we were taken in. You pilchard."

"I didn't say anything about the cardboard legs, though."

"You didn't have to," Graham snapped, striding out so that he left Nathan behind.

Once inside the building, he saw Beth at the end of a queue waiting outside the science labs, and sidled up to her.

"Wotcher," she said and the two girls in front of her turned and looked Graham up and down.

"Yes," said Graham. "Hello. Look…"

"What?"

"About Saturday … I didn't mean to … I mean I'm sorry if I was a bit harsh…"

"Oh, that's all right."

"Only you know how it is…"

"I know. It doesn't matter."

She gave him one of her broad, shiny smiles, and he saw that it really didn't matter. She'd forgotten all about it. There'd probably been no need to apologize at all.

"Tell you what, though," she said, dropping her voice to a loud whisper and taking his arm. "I've had another thought."

"What about?"

"What we can do. The Anti-Noodles."

"We? I haven't said you're in yet, have I?"

"I must be in, Graham, because I've already helped you out, and Vicki said…"

"The Anti-Noodles is my idea, not Vicki's."

The two girls in front of Beth were still staring at him. He turned his back to them.

"I just wanted to say sorry about Saturday, that's all," he said.

"It's all right. I told you it's all right. Do you want to hear my new idea?"

"No, thanks."

"There's a drama group and they're putting on a play. They want a team to put all the stuff on."

"Stuff?"

"Yes. Tables and stuff."

"The set."

"That's right. Why don't we do it? As a team."

"No, thanks."

"Go on. It's a brilliant idea. We can be in the programme. 'The stuff was moved on and off by the Anti-Noodles.'"

"Listen, Beth," sighed Graham. "How do you know about this?"

"I can't remember. Someone told me…"

"Exactly. Just like someone told Vicky about Leggy leaving. How do you know it's not a wind-up?"

"Because there really is a drama group. A bloke from our form's going to be in this play. Bloke with glasses. What's his name?"

"No. Really. We're not getting caught out twice."

The line began to shuffle into the labs.

"OK, Graham," Beth said, backing away. "You think about it. I'll see you in the sandwich room and we can make our plans."

"No. Can't you hear what I'm saying, you dim-wit!"

"Got to go now, Gray! See you later."

She was like some armoured vehicle, ploughing straight through whatever stood in her way, barbs and insults bouncing off her, deaf to all common sense.

And Gray! Nobody called him Gray. Unless they wanted to insult him.

I'll have to get hold of Nathan before she does, he thought, or he'll fall for this daft idea and we'll end up looking like idiots again.

In the sandwich room, Mr Trainor's head was resting on his hand and his eyes were closed over his pile of books.

"Listen," Graham said, sliding next to Nathan, who gazed fixedly at the Greek posters and chewed a sausage roll. "I've had a word with Beth..."

"Ah, Graham. It's you. I've had a thought."

"Well, I'm really pleased for you, Nathan, but will you just listen to me for a moment? I've seen Beth and she's got this idea..."

"Did you say sorry? About the way you

went on at her?"

"What? Yes. Just let me finish, will you? She'll be in here in a minute and there'll be no stopping her. She's got this mad idea about the drama group..."

"Actually, that's how I got my idea."

"The drama group? You haven't seen her already, have you?"

"No. My idea about Beth. It came from this way she has of getting herself involved..."

"Yes. Wonderful. But I have to tell you what she's come up with next. If you're not forewarned she'll make you think it's a brilliant idea and before we know it—"

"Well, maybe it is a brilliant idea."

"No, Nathan, it isn't. She wants us to move the set for the drama group."

"What, you and me?"

"The Anti-Noodles. And it's a really stupid idea."

"Is it? Why?"

"Because quite probably it's a scam. Like those stupid legs the Noodles—"

"Ah!"

"Ah? What do you mean, ah?"

"This is where my idea comes in."

Graham blinked at him. It was unusual for Nathan to come up with any kind of idea, and for a moment he was thrown.

"You reckon one of the Noodles has got to her, do you?" Nathan went on. "I agree.

That's quite possible. And that's what I was thinking. Why don't we get Beth to join the Noodles?"

"Because she doesn't *want* to join the Noodles. She said she didn't."

"No, no. You don't get it, Graham. Not actually join them. *Pretend* to join them."

"Why?"

"Well, that's the beauty of it. Then she can act as a spy."

"A spy?"

"Yes. So she can tell us what they're up to."

"No."

"Why not?"

"Because she's not a proper member of the Anti-Noodles, and she can't spy if she's not a proper member."

Nathan took another slow bite of sausage roll.

"Oh," he said. "I sort of thought she was."

The door crashed open and Beth came in beaming.

"Wotcher, you two! Have you told him about my idea, Graham?"

"About the drama group?" said Nathan. "Yes. I didn't quite see what the point was, though."

"We'd move the stuff on and off."

"Stuff?"

"She means the set," said Graham.

"That's right," Beth said, dumping her

lunch box on the table next to them. "It's something for us to do. You know, like Vicki said, something useful and sensible."

"It isn't really," Graham began, "because I don't think—"

"I get it," Nathan said. "Kind of team-work."

"Yes. And they could put us in the programme. The whassname – set – moved on and off by the Anti-Noodles."

Graham sighed again and clenched his fists. He could feel things slipping away from him.

"Good idea," said Nathan. "I like it."

"I knew you'd come round to it in the end," Beth said sweetly to Graham. "Want a crisp?"

"No. Thanks."

"I'm glad you think it's a good idea, Graham, because I've already had a word with Jason."

"Jason? Who the hell's Jason?"

Talking to Beth was like playing table tennis with Toby. You soon learned not to expect the ball to come back over the net. It was just as likely to ping off the light shade.

"Jason's the bloke I was telling you about. The one in the drama group. He said he'd have a word with Mrs Backhouse but it would probably be all right. There's a meeting in the hall at three this afternoon. I told him we'd be there."

* * *

As it turned out, the set-moving scheme was a genuine one. Mrs Backhouse was at the meeting handing out scripts to would-be actors, and there wasn't a Noodle in sight. All the same, Graham decided to stay in the background and say as little as possible, so he lodged himself between two piles of chairs at the side of the hall and watched.

"Now," said Mrs Backhouse. "*The Tempest.*"

Mrs Backhouse had a clear and precise voice which swooped on certain words with particular relish.

"*The Tempest,*" she said, "by William *Shakespeare*. It's a particularly..."

"I know about him," Beth chipped in.

"Good, good..."

"We done one of his shows at our last school. I was a moth."

Very appropriate, thought Graham. Very like a moth. Better still, a wasp. "And you want to be in this one, do you, Beth?" Mrs Backhouse asked, smiling like someone sucking a sweet.

"Oh, no. I'm here to move the stuff."

"Stuff?"

"Get the tables and chairs on and off, miss."

"Ah, the *set*. Well, there are no tables and chairs in this play – it's set on an island – but there are *rocks* and trees and things, so we'll need a good stage *crew*."

"That's us then, miss," said Beth. "The Anti-Noodles."

"The what?"

"Anti-Noodles, miss. It's a sort of club what does useful things."

"Yes. I see."

Graham shrank deeper into the shadow of the chairs. Hearing Beth pipe out the name like that made it sound like some kind of play-school activity. The sort of thing big floppy puppets got you to join in with when you were about four.

"My dad lives on an island at the moment, actually," Beth added, turning to the assembled company. "In Africa. He sends me post-cards so I can tell you just what an island would really be like. The kinds of trees and things..."

"Well, that could prove useful," said Mrs Backhouse, with another sweet-sucking smile, "but, if you don't mind, we ought to get on with the *play*."

"Right-oh, miss. Press on."

Mrs Backhouse pressed on, describing each character in turn and spouting chunks of the play with her eyes shut. The would-be actors thumbed through the scripts, counting lines.

"Ah, *Graham*," she said, suddenly squinting into the gloom where he crouched. "You've come for a part, have you? Jolly good."

"Not really, miss..."

"No? Are you sure? Because I could see you as Caliban."

"I'm here to help backstage."

"That's right, miss," said Beth. "He's with us. One of the Anti-Noodles."

"Really?"

A smile played at the corners of Mrs Backhouse's lips.

"Who is Caliban anyway?" Beth asked.

"He's a sort of wild creature who lives on the island."

Beth looked at Graham and snorted.

"A wild creature!" she laughed. "Oh no, I don't think that's Graham."

"I just want to help with the set, that's all," said Graham, feeling his cheeks burning.

No, I don't, he thought. I don't want anything at all to do with this. So why am I saying that I do?

"Of course," said Mrs Backhouse. "Of course. Helping with the set. And very necessary that will be. Welcome aboard, Graham."

While they were waiting for French to start, Graham rested his head on his desk and stared blankly at the wall.

"How does she do these things?" he muttered to himself. "And why can't we ever stop her?"

Nathan looked down at him, wondering whether this was a good time to say what was on his mind. Probably not, he thought, but it would have to be said anyway. After a moment or two he said casually, "You remember what we were saying about the spying?"

"About what?"

"The spying idea. Remember?"

Graham lifted an eyebrow in Nathan's direction. He looked like a bored dog in its basket.

"No."

"Yes you do. About Beth becoming one of the Noodles and—"

"Oh, that. Yes. Why?"

"Well, I was thinking," said Nathan, looking vaguely out of the window. "It might just work."

"Of course it wouldn't work, Nathan. Nothing to do with Beth works. I bet her house is full of things that don't work. Clocks and toasters and..."

"But with a bit of thought and planning..."

"No, it's a bad idea. Save energy and stop thinking about it."

"Ah," said Nathan.

Graham sat up sharply.

"What have you done?" he asked.

"I haven't actually *done* anything, Graham."

"You didn't mention it to her, did you?"

"No. No, of course not. No, Graham, I didn't. No."

"No?"

"Slightly, yes."

"What do you mean 'slightly'?"

"She sort of got me talking about it. I don't know how. I never meant to talk about it, honest, but she worms things out of you..."

"We've got to stop her, Nathan. She can't be a spy. If she starts charging around like a pint-sized James Bond..."

"She might not. She might just forget about it."

Graham gave him a pitying look.

"I can assure you, Nathan, she certainly will not forget about it..."

He would have said more but just then Vicki dropped into the desk behind them.

"What news on the Noodle front?" she asked.

"All quiet, as far as I can tell," said Nathan, glad of the interruption. "What about you?"

"Nothing," she said. "I was in History with Peter Smith and George, but they were just keeping their heads down."

"Doing what?" said Graham.

"Writing, I think."

"Writing? Smith was writing? Well, that's unusual for a start. I bet they're up to something."

Shortly after the last bell of the day, Graham found out what it was the Noodles were up to. People were milling about on the steps outside the main doors and Peter Smith was addressing them, using a rolled-up magazine as a megaphone. George Marriott was handing out leaflets to passers-by.

"Leaflets," Graham said to Vicki out of the corner of his mouth. "That's what they were writing."

"What do they want leaflets for?"

Smith's voice came booming over their heads.

"The Way Ahead – The Noodle Way. Is your life dull and meaningless? Do you wonder what it's all about? Then join the Noodle Party. The party of the people. You know it makes no sense!"

George Marriott wove his way through the crowd and thrust a leaflet into Graham's hand.

"Join the Noodle Party, sir?"

"The Noodle *Party*?" echoed Graham.

"Yes, sir. You know it makes no sense."

"Then why would I want to join?" said Graham, shoving the leaflet back at George.

"It could change your life, sir. We plan to hold weekly parliaments, you know."

"Really? How fascinating."

"Dead right it is. But only on Wednesdays." He tucked the leaflet down the front of Graham's jacket and moved on to someone else. Peter Smith, meanwhile, was warming to his theme.

"Ladies and gentlemen, in the election of life

are you going to put your cross against the box marked fun, or are you going to vote for boredom? A vote for Noodles is a vote for fun. And remember, if you would be so kind –" he added, waving his arms dramatically – "a Noodle is not just for Christmas! A Noodle is for life!"

"I've had enough of this," Graham said.

He put his head down and elbowed his way through the crowd towards the gates.

"What about our next meeting?" Vicki called after him.

"Tomorrow. Six o'clock, in the shed!" he shouted over his shoulder.

He caught sight of Smith, still bellowing away on the school steps. Briefly their eyes met. Smith stopped in mid-sentence and pointed at him.

"There, ladies and gentlemen!" he yelled. "There he goes, look! Graham Keefe! The leader of the opposition. Be warned, be warned! If you're not with the Noodles, you're with the Anti-Noodles, and the Anti-Noodles look like that! I know, it's sad, but you don't want to end up like that, do you, ladies and gentlemen?"

For a second Graham considered shouting back, but he couldn't think of anything sharp enough or witty enough. He could never find the right words at moments like that. Sometimes he found them later, in the dark hours of the night when there was no one around to hear him, but when it mattered his mind seized up and his tongue became thick in his mouth.

By the time he reached the gates, sweat was trickling down the inside of his shirt and his cheeks were glowing with humiliation. Once he'd gained the safety of the public highway, well out of sight and ear-shot, he slowed down, loosened his jacket and flapped his shirt to get some air to his body. Something fluttered to his feet. He picked it up.

He saw a crude sketch of someone with sticking-up hair and a mass of badges on his lapels. It was him. Even though he only had two badges on his jacket, he knew it was supposed to be him. He felt slightly sick. There was a caption beneath the sketch.

The leader of the opposition. G. Keefe, Anti-Noodle. A sad case. A danger to us all. Vote Noodle and help to stamp him out.

Graham screwed the paper up, threw it violently into the hedge and stalked off. A moment or two later he retraced his steps and groped about to get it back. No use leaving it around for all and sundry to find, he thought. He was crouching with his arm deep inside the hedge when someone spoke behind him.

"You lost something?"

His fingers closed on the leaflet and he twisted round to squint up at the voice. It was Beth's sister, Amanda. She was looking down at him with her bag slung over her shoulder. The look on her face combined puzzlement and contempt.

"No," said Graham, hauling himself up. "No, I was just..."

"What?"

"You know. Just ... I thought I saw something. In the hedge. But I didn't."

She continued to look at him, unsmilingly, and he screwed the leaflet up and slipped it into his pocket.

"Well," he said, "I'd better be off, I suppose."

"Hang on a minute," she said. "I'm not standing here because I like watching nerds fighting hedges. I want a word with you."

"Me? Why?"

"What do you want with our Beth?"

What did he want with her? He didn't want anything. He wanted her to go away and leave him in peace. He opened his mouth to say so, and thought better of it. Amanda was studying him with her dark and lovely eyes. Dark and a bit dangerous, it seemed to him.

"What's this club thing she's been going on about?" she said.

"Club thing?"

"She says you've started a club. What is it?"

"Nothing really. I mean..."

"It can't be nothing. She gabs on about it all the time. What's it called?"

"Well, it hasn't got a proper name. Not really. We just call it – " he looked away, focusing vaguely on something in the distance – "the Anti-Noodles," he mumbled.

"The what?"

"Anti-Noodles."

It came out louder than he meant it to. He made a sort of hopeless gesture, flapping his arms.

"Yes, I thought that's what she said. Only it sounded too barmy to be true."

"Yes, well, it is in a way," said Graham, trying to laugh. "It's just, you know, a bit of fun."

"You're not taking the rise out of her, are you?"

"Good Lord, no!"

"Only, I know she's a bit of a pain at times, but I wouldn't want anyone taking the rise out of her."

"No, no. It's as I say, a bit of fun. She wanted to join and I said she could. Happy to have her with us. You know. Good old Beth."

"Right. Keep it that way, then."

She studied him a moment longer and then turned to leave. Before she'd gone more than a few paces he called after her – "Excuse me!" – and almost immediately wished he hadn't. She stopped and looked back at him.

"Can I ask...?" he began.

"What?"

"Beth was telling us about her dad. I was just wondering..."

She took a step or two closer to him and narrowed those dark eyes.

"Wondering what?"

"He's in Africa, is he?"

"Africa?"

"That's what Beth said."

"If that's what she said, he must be, mustn't he?"

"Yes, of course."

"But I wouldn't wonder too much about it, if I were you, Keith," she said, "because it really isn't any of your business."

To begin with Graham wasn't going to tell Nathan about his encounter with Amanda. After all, he'd been threatened by a girl and he felt rather pathetic about that. Of course, she hadn't actually said anything particularly threatening. It was more her manner, and those dark, hard eyes which so unnerved him. And there'd been something decidedly cagey about what she'd said when he'd mentioned Beth's father being in Africa. She hadn't said he was, and she hadn't said he wasn't. And Graham wanted a second opinion on that, so during the next lunch break he steered Nathan into a quiet corner of Yard Two. They leaned side by side against the gym wall, with their hands in their pockets, watching half a dozen short boys thundering up and down after a punctured ball.

"Well, well," Nathan said, and he whistled softly through his teeth. "Amanda, eh?"

"Yes. It was a bit odd, if you know what I mean."

"Very nice, though. There must've been something – you know – exciting about it. I mean, Amanda..."

"I thought she was going to pop me one, if that's what you mean."

"Even so. I mean, Amanda."

"Yes, yes. Amanda. You've got the picture. But what was she getting at?"

"Wish I'd been there."

"Nathan. What was she getting at, do you think?"

"How should I know? Just warning you off, I expect. Maybe Beth told her about the way you went on at her..."

"No, there's more to it than that. That stuff about Africa. What do you reckon that was about?"

"Well, possibly Beth was making that up, only Amanda didn't want to let you know she was making it up."

Graham bit his lip and thought for a moment or two.

"Yes," he said. "That's what I thought. But why should she do that?"

"He's probably not in Africa at all. He's

probably somewhere else. Somewhere not so glamorous. Like Belgium. Or Hull..."

"Hull?"

"Yes. If your old man was in Hull you wouldn't go around telling everyone, would you?"

"I suppose not. But I wouldn't go around saying he was in Africa either."

"Well, you're not Beth," said Nathan with an air of finality. "I should forget about it if I were you. Unless you want Amanda to slap you around. Which you might, of course. I must say, I wouldn't mind."

"You surprise me at times, Nathan. You wander around half asleep, and then you come out with all this weird stuff about wanting to be slapped around by Beth's sister."

"That's not weird, Graham. That's perfectly natural. Anyway, I'm not saying I want to get *beaten up* exactly. It's just that a bit of light slapping might be..."

"Yes, all right. Don't go on about it. I just want to know what you think."

"I think forget it. There's more pressing matters to concern us."

"Like what?"

"The Anti-Noodle Set-Shifting Team."

"The play, you mean?"

Graham sighed and ran his fingers through his hair. He didn't want anything to do with the play. He couldn't see how moving cardboard rocks about was going to help the Anti-Noodle cause. And anyway it hadn't been his idea. It was something he'd been pushed into doing. By Beth. With Nathan's help.

"There's a meeting in the hall," said Nathan. "In five minutes."

"Really?"

"For all concerned."

"Well, I'm not concerned."

"You said you were. You more or less promised..."

That was the trouble. Graham *had* more or less promised, so he couldn't just not go. With a roll of his eyes, he heaved himself away from the gym wall and trudged across the yard. When they got to the hall, the actors were gathered in murmuring groups, flicking through their scripts.

"Arty-farty," mumbled Graham. "Be honest. It's not really us, is it?"

"Set-shifting isn't arty-farty. It's manual work."

Beth was also there, talking furiously at Mrs Backhouse as she tried to arrange chairs to look like an island. When she saw Graham and Nathan, she gave them a cheery wave and skipped over to say hello.

"Did Nathe tell you?" she asked Graham.

"Tell me what?"

"About my spying idea."

"Your idea?" said Nathan.

"Yes, don't you remember? We had a talk about it."

"Well, I think we need to have another talk about it," Graham said. "Later. And don't do a thing until we have talked."

"Right-oh, boss."

He scowled at her, then grasped his thigh and limped over to Mrs Backhouse.

"I'll just sort of watch, if that's all right with you," he said. "Only I've done my leg in and I can't move much..."

"There's nothing *to* move at this stage, *Graham*. This is the first rehearsal."

"Oh. Then perhaps..."

He winced and began to limp back to the door.

"No, don't go. It'll be useful for your team to see what we have in mind."

His team? They weren't his team.

"Actually, Mrs Backhouse," he said, "I'm not supposed to lift heavy weights..."

"Don't *worry* about it. You've got a month to get fit. Just sit and watch."

He gave her a weak smile, then hauled himself to the side of the hall, where he slid down the wall and sat on the floor with his leg at full stretch. Beth skipped after him.

"What's up with you, Graham?" she said.

"Nothing," he muttered.

"But you look crocked."

"I don't want to move any set, that's all."

"Why?"

"Because it's a daft idea and I've got better things to do with my life, that's why."

"So you haven't got a wonky leg?"

"No."

Her eyes widened and she half turned to say something to Mrs Backhouse.

"No, Beth," he added quickly. "Don't tell her, for goodness' sake."

"So you mean, the limp and everything is *acting*? Wow."

"Yes. But just keep quiet about it, will you?"

"You're really good, you know, Graham. I thought you'd done your leg in for sure. You ought to be *in* the play..."

"Beth..."

"It would be good for us, wouldn't it? Good publicity."

"We don't want any kind of publicity, thank you. And I keep telling you, you're not..."

"Can we make a start, *please*?" called Mrs Backhouse, clapping her hands.

The actors gathered round and Beth skipped back to make sure she wasn't missing anything.

"Bit of a problem to begin with, I'm afraid," announced Mrs Backhouse. "We've lost our Caliban."

"Oh no," Beth piped. "What a nuisance."

"So our first task is to find another one."

"I'll go for you, miss, if you like."

"Go, Beth? Go where?"

"To get another what's-its-name. If you just tell me where..."

"No, Beth. Caliban is not a thing. It's a person. A character. Which means we're an actor short."

"Oh no!"

"So if any of you know someone who might be *persuaded* to try..."

"To be an actor, miss? I know someone."

Mrs Backhouse looked frowningly at her for a moment.

"Are you sure?"

"Oh yes," nodded Beth. "And he's very good. I *know* he's very good."

And she turned and looked across the hall directly at Graham.

SPIES

That afternoon, when Graham trailed into the Humanities Room with the rest of his form, he was reunited with the swimming trunks. They were steaming again so the phantom swimmer had obviously been for another dip. Graham regarded them with disgust. Draped casually and gaudily on the radiator as they were, they seemed, somehow, to mock him.

All my problems spring from these damn things, he thought. The start of the Noodles. Their stupid election leaflets. A whole string of things, each of them beyond his control. And now a part in a play. If ever there was ammunition for the Noodles, it was a part in a play.

Graham Keefe as Caliban.

A wild creature who behaved, according to Mrs Backhouse, much as the Noodles behaved.

Of course, there was also that maggot of a

girl. Deep down Graham knew that there was, in fact, no connection between the steaming trunks and Beth – or none that he could discern – but at the moment it *felt* as if the trunks were responsible for her too. As if they were winking colourfully at him:

"Hi, Gray. How goes it? You're an actor now, we hear. A wild man. Should be good for a laugh..."

Suddenly he snatched them up and flung them across the room. They slapped against the wall, clung there for a second, and flopped behind a desk. Briefly he felt a surge of satisfaction. Then he noticed Miss Garden standing at the door watching him.

"Not the trunks again, Graham, please," she said.

"Sorry, miss. They were in my way..."

He edged apologetically towards them but she stopped him.

"No, leave them alone. They've ruined one lesson. I'm not allowing them to ruin another. Stay where you are."

"It's strange behaviour, though, isn't it, miss?" said Peter Smith, sitting, arms folded, near the front. "For one who appears so normal."

Miss Garden dumped her books on the table and turned to level an icy gaze at him.

"Have you completed that detention?" she asked.

"Yes, miss. Thank you, miss."

"Then I suggest you don't court another. Keep your opinions to yourself."

"I'm only saying, miss," he persisted, "he claims to be an Anti-Noodle but..."

"A what?"

"An Anti-Noodle, miss. You know. The Reasonable Party."

She hesitated and Graham could see flickering across her face both curiosity and a distinct reluctance to become further embroiled.

Don't ask, he thought. For your sake and mine, please don't ask.

"I'm afraid you've lost me," she said. "Anti-Noodles? What is all this?"

"It's a kind of experiment in democracy," said Smith. "A bit like a general election, you know. People have to make their minds up who they choose to follow. That's why I thought you might be interested, miss."

"Well, of course I am interested in that, Peter," said Miss Garden. "People making decisions. Moral responsibility..."

Graham could see a chasm of difficulties opening before them.

"I shouldn't bother if I were you, miss," he cut in. "It doesn't really make any sense."

"No, Graham. Give Peter a chance. He's talking about choice, and how we all make choices is of vital importance."

"But he's a Noodle, miss."

"And you shouldn't make choices by sticking rude labels on people."

"I didn't make the label. You did..."

"I did? What are you talking about?"

"You called him a Noodle, when you gave him that detention, and it kind of stuck."

Miss Garden perched thoughtfully on the edge of her table and put her hands together, fingertip to fingertip.

"Oh dear, I think perhaps you're right," she said, then she turned to Smith. "I'm sorry, Peter. No doubt it was said in the heat of the moment. I never intended you to be known as a noodle for the rest of your time here."

Peter Smith made a dismissive gesture and smiled pleasantly at her.

"That's OK, miss. Actually, you did me a favour."

"How so?"

"Well, you kind of hit the nail on the head. I realized I *was* a noodle, you see, and that I didn't mind being a noodle. Being a noodle sort of stood for all the things I believed in. So I became a Noodle with a capital *N*, if you see what I mean."

"Really?"

"Oh yes. So did a lot of people. George here is a Noodle, aren't you, George?"

"Only on Wednesdays," said Marriott.

"What?"

"Don't worry about that, miss," Smith

explained. "He means yes."

"But you mentioned Anti-Noodles. And the Reasonable Party..."

"Yes, miss. The Anti-Noodles are the opposition, if you like. And we call them the Reasonable Party because that's what they think they are."

"Well, we are," said Graham. "What's wrong with that?"

Miss Garden frowned at him, full of interest.

"Ah," she said. "So you're an Anti-Noodle, are you, Graham?"

"Yes, but really, miss, it's not that important..."

"But it is, Graham. You should have the courage of your convictions. Are you the only one? Is anyone else here an Anti-Noodle?"

She looked round the room but there was no response. Nathan was staring out of the window. He was listening – Graham knew he was listening – but he'd somehow managed to make his face look even more vacant than usual.

"Come on, Nathan," Graham said. "You're one too."

"Hmm?"

"An Anti-Noodle."

"Well ... sort of..."

"He is. And so is Vicki."

"And what's the point?" asked Miss

Garden. "I mean, what do you actually *do*? Nathan?"

Nathan pursed his lips and thought.

"Do you do anything?"

"Oh, yes," he said. "We do. I just can't think for the moment... Oh, yes. We did these cards..."

"Ah-ha!" said George Marriott suddenly.

"No we didn't," Graham put in. "We saw through that, if you remember."

"No. We didn't do the cards. That's right. We didn't..."

"Well, that's something you didn't do," said Miss Garden. "Which all sounds rather vague. What about the Noodles? What do they do?"

"Perhaps you'd like to peruse our literature, miss," said Peter Smith, leaning forward and handing her a leaflet.

She glanced at it, looked up at Graham, and stifled a grin.

"I'm also baking a Noodle cake," Smith went on. "To go in the Display of Work next month. One of my specials. We're kind of free spirits, see. We do whatever comes into our heads, whereas Keefe and the others simply follow instructions. They have closed minds..."

"At least we've got minds to be closed," snapped Graham.

"All right, all right," said Miss Garden. "Let's not descend to insults."

"What about that leaflet, though? That's insulting. As a teacher you ought to put a stop to that sort of thing."

"Well, maybe you're right," she said. "But basically what we've got here are two very different approaches to life. One that celebrates silliness – be young and carefree while you have the chance – and another that follows the path of sense. And what Peter is doing is asking people to choose between the two."

"I know," said Graham, "but it's stupid. Who's going to choose to be silly?"

"Lots of people already have," Smith told him.

"More fool them!"

"Exactly. But they don't care."

"That's just selfish!"

"Calm down," said Miss Garden. "If you want people to behave reasonably, Graham, you have to persuade them that it's a good idea. What we need here, I think, is an *actual* election, with speeches by both parties, so that people can make up their own minds."

"Brilliant," said Smith immediately. "You're on!"

For the second time that day Graham felt trapped. The last thing he wanted was to get into a debate – not with slippery, smooth-tongued Smith – but there was a rumble of interest from the rest of the form, and Miss Garden was obviously keen on the idea.

"Come on, then, Graham," she said. "A proper debate. Come out here and tell us why we should be sensible. Then we'll hear from Peter."

Graham, his head swimming, dragged himself to the front. Half an hour ago he'd learned that he was to become a wild savage in a play, and now he was a political leader. Miss Garden held up her hand for silence and he looked at the rows of waiting faces.

"The thing is," he said hesitantly, "I mean, what we believe is that ... well, you can't just go around making a complete dork of yourself, can you?"

"Give it up, then!" called out Smith, and everyone laughed.

"Not me. You. Because we live in a society, right? We have to get along with other people, whatever they're like. We have to do our bit to help –"

He paused. The words he wanted to say trod about heavily inside his head and kept getting out of order. He couldn't muster them as he needed to.

This is sounding pathetic, he thought. I'm not saying what I mean. I don't even *know* what I mean...

"The Anti-Noodles are just about ... well, trying to act responsibly."

"Oh, yes," said Smith, turning to appeal to the others. "Like inventing a school pig."

"That was to pay you back for treading on my cake!"

"Don't get me wrong, Keefe. I didn't *mind* the pig thing. I just don't see how you can call it responsible."

"Well, maybe it wasn't but I'm not going to sit back while a bunch of idiots go around stamping on people's cakes..."

"Hang on, hang on," said Miss Garden. "I'm losing track again. What have pigs and cake got to do with all this?"

"It doesn't matter, miss," Graham said. "That's history now. All I'm saying is that we have to prepare ourselves to be useful members of society. The Noodles don't do that. They just act like air-heads and I think that's only going to lead to ... to—"

"Locking them up!" called out George Marriott and everyone laughed again.

Graham looked hopelessly from face to grinning face. Then he gave up and sat down. Peter Smith took his place but didn't speak for some moments. He waited for quiet, and when he had it, he waited a little longer, staring round the room and smiling.

"I only have one thing to tell you," he said at last in a controlled voice. "Perhaps you've heard the old proverb: It's better to spend one day as a tiger than forty years as a sheep? No? Then think about it now. The Noodles want to be tigers. The Anti-Noodles are already sheep. And that, ladies and gentlemen, is all we are about. I thank you."

He gave a little bow and sat down. There was a moment's silence, then cheering and stamping for almost a minute. Miss Garden called for quiet and said that in a week or so they'd put it to a vote; meanwhile they could persuade people to support them, as long as things didn't get out of hand. Graham kept his eyes on the table top, feeling silly and small. As they filed out at the end of the lesson, Nathan fell in beside him.

"I thought you talked a lot of sense," he said. "Thanks."

"When it comes to it, people will vote for us, I'm sure. That new bloke with the glasses already said he would."

"Really?"

"And Vicki will. So it's kind of building up, isn't it?"

"Actually, Nathan, it's kind of pathetic – you, Vicki and the new bloke with glasses. It's hardly a throng, is it? In fact, at the moment everything that could go wrong has gone wrong. It's the end of a really bad day, and that's all you can say."

But he was wrong about that. It wasn't quite the end. When he got home later that afternoon, he found Beth waiting for him in the shed.

* * *

There was no sign of Mum or Toby when he got in, so he made himself a mug of tea and stood at the French windows staring into the garden as the evening gloom descended. The humiliations and failures of the day swirled around in his head and he closed his eyes to clear them. When he opened them again, he saw the shed door move and a short arm appear. It flicked something at the bushes and went in again.

"It can't be," he said to himself. "It just can't be."

But he held his breath and peered hard down the garden. A small round head bobbed across the murk of the shed window. Graham banged down his mug and stormed up the garden path. He flung open the shed door. She was humming to herself and arranging daisies in a row of flowerpots on a shelf.

"Oh, there you are," she said over her shoulder. "I was wondering where you'd got to."

"What the hell are you doing here?"

"Just making it look nice. There was some dried up old bulb things so I chucked them out and got flowers instead."

"They were Dad's onions."

"Well, he wouldn't want them, Graham. They were dead. It looks much better like this."

He breathed through his nose, in then out, hard.

"Beth," he said, "what are you doing here?"

"I've come for the meeting."

"What meeting? There is no meeting."

"I thought you said there was."

"I never said a word, you soft bag! How did you get in?"

"The door wasn't locked..."

"How did you get in the garden?"

"Oh. Over the back gate. There was no one about so I had to."

She stood aside and indicated her row of wilting daisies.

"Nice, aren't they?" she said. "They're only daisies, though. I got them off of the lawn so I don't think anyone will mind..."

"You can't do this, Beth. You can't just turn up at people's houses."

He paused as a chilling new thought occurred to him.

"Does your sister know you're here?" he asked.

"No."

"Well, don't tell her. I don't think she'd like it."

"I wasn't going to tell her anyway. You can't go around telling people things like that."

"Like what? What are you talking about?"

"Spying and things. You don't *tell* people you're a spy, do you? Otherwise they'd all..."

"Who said you were a spy?"

"You did."

"No!"

"Didn't you? I thought you said..."

"I said we'd talk about it. Later."

Graham heard a door slam in the house and darted to the shed window. He could see a square of yellow light in the kitchen, and his mother moving about, probably making tea. She was early. She never usually got back this early. He turned back to Beth and made her sit on the grassbox of the lawnmower and keep her head down.

"Mum's back," he said. "So you can't go now. She'll see you. And we don't want that, do we?"

"Why don't we want that, Graham?"

Because you're so small and embarrassing, he thought. Because I'd cringe with shame if they knew you were down here.

"Because spies can't be popping up all over the place, can they?" he said. "The point of spies is that they're *not* seen."

"So I *am* a spy?"

"What? Yes, yes. Just keep your head down."

She ducked her head, then wriggled her shoulders and grinned.

"Good this, isn't it?" she said.

Graham glowered at her and didn't answer. He told her to stay still and quiet until he came back. Then he'd find a way of sneaking her out unseen. He inched open the shed door and peered out.

"Graham?"

"What now?"

"Before I sneak off home, I'll tell you about my first meeting, shall I?"

"What first meeting?"

"With Smith's lot," she said. "When I joined the Noodles."

"You've joined them already?" he said incredulously.

"Oh yes."

"But we said ... I told you..."

He stared at her with his mouth open for several seconds. He felt like shouting at her but there really wasn't much point.

"Later, Beth," he said. "Tell me later."

Then he nipped out of the shed and slunk up the garden like a cat.

It was almost half an hour before he could return, and darkness had settled over the garden. He took a torch with him but didn't switch it on until he was inside the shed. The beam struck Beth's face and she screwed up her eyes. She was still sitting on the grassbox, her hands on her knees.

"You can go now," he said. "They're in the front room watching telly."

"All of them?"

"Mum and Toby."

"Where's your dad?"

"He's at work. He doesn't get back till seven."

"But he doesn't have far to go, does he? I mean, the prison's only just over the road, isn't it? Has he got a bike?"

"Yes. Look, it doesn't matter. We haven't got time to discuss how my dad gets to work..."

"All right. Next time, then."

He grabbed her arm, hustled her out of the shed and pointed her up the garden.

"The side alley," he said. "Go on, off you go, and keep your head down."

She set off at a crouching run, swinging her arms as she went. He watched until she'd disappeared into the shadows at the side of the house, then went back into the shed and shone the torch around. It would be just like Beth to leave some incriminating evidence behind – a hair-band or something, or, knowing her, a notebook with her name in it. My Spying Notebook by Beth Rayburn.

He saw nothing; just a dusty patch on the floorboards where she'd fidgeted her feet about while she was waiting for him. He smoothed it over, switched off the torch and returned to the house.

The more he thought about the forthcoming election, the more determined Graham became that the Anti-Noodles would win it. He could see what stood in their way, though: their public image was rather vague and uninspiring; some might even say boring. He was brooding on this when he went to the next rehearsal of *The Tempest*. Mrs Backhouse started by talking through the characters – what drove them, what they wanted and where they were coming from.

"Caliban, for example," she said, looking at the earnest group which encircled her. "In many ways he's the most *interesting* character in the play. He acts like a beast but he speaks like an angel. This is fascinating, don't you think?"

"Hmm," Graham said.

"What does he *want*, do you think, Graham?"

Graham stroked his chin and tried to look like someone pondering. He glanced at the others for help and noticed that Beth was there too. He didn't know *why* she was there: there was still no set to move. She was sitting on the edge of her seat with her hand up.

"I think I know, miss."

"I was meaning the actors, actually, Beth..."

"He wants to be left alone, miss."

He's not the only one, thought Graham.

After several more minutes of talk about the characters, Mrs Backhouse got them to push their chairs back and walk around the hall.

"In character, mind," she called. "Walk as your character might walk."

She turned a blind eye to the fact that Beth was a scene-shifter: it was easier to keep quiet and let her join in. Graham broke into a half-hearted shuffle.

"More beast-like, Graham, if you can!"

He hunched his shoulders and let his mouth drop open.

"Better. Much better!"

He gnashed his teeth and rolled his eyes.

"Oh, *splendid*! Lovely!"

Then he began to relax into the role and set off with more purpose, lurching violently and moaning. He thought that perhaps this was a start – a way of making the Anti-Noodles more *interesting* – but when he reached the doors at the top of the hall, he saw Peter Smith and Angela Carr staring at him through the glass.

"Damn," he said.

"No dialogue, please," called Mrs Backhouse. "Just movement."

He straightened up and tried to look normal. The two Noodles exchanged sorrowful glances – "how sad, how very sad" – and then moved slowly off, shaking their heads.

"Keep moving, keep moving!" Mrs Backhouse shouted.

Graham looked round at the rest of the

group. Beth was storming round the hall with an expression of deep concentration on her face. She moved in the same crouching, arm-swinging way that Graham had seen the night before in his garden, and was coming straight for him. He sidestepped. She sidestepped.

"Whoops," she said, bouncing into him.

"What did you do that for, you little idiot?"

"Sorry, Gray. Didn't see you coming."

But he was sure that she *had* seen him coming. And now she was nodding at the floor with one eye closed. Graham looked down and saw a square of folded paper.

"Oh, dear," she said very precisely. "You've dropped something."

"No, I haven't..."

"I think you have, Graham. You'd better pick it up. It looks important."

By this time several of the others had slowed down and were looking at them. Graham stooped and picked the paper up. Beth gave him a little thumbs-up sign and went beetling off at her crouching run again.

Nathan had waited outside during the rehearsal, and walked back to the house with Graham afterwards. Mum was still at the library and Toby was with his noisy friend Barry, so as usual they had the place to themselves for a while. Graham took a couple of cans from the fridge and set them down on the kitchen table. Then he unfolded the paper and spread it out in front of Nathan.

"What's this?"

"It's from Beth. A report on her spying activities."

"Spying? I thought she said she was going to wait before..."

"She *said* she was, yes. You'd better read it."

First report on the Noodles, it said. *From Anti-Noodle agent, code name Rasputin...*

"Rasputin?" said Nathan. "Where did she come by that name?"

"Who knows?"

Nathan read on.

I went to this meeting in Yard 2. It might not of been a proper meeting but there was a lot of Noodles there anyway. They told me to buzz off but i said i wanted to join the Noodles and they didn't bother after that. They talked a lot of rubbish most of the time and Peter Smith (code name Dracular) was telling us about the cake what he is making for the Display of Work and how it is going to have a Noodle design on it in icing. Then they went on about the play. They said that Graham (code name Leonardo) was going to be in it. Then they said some other things about him and they all laughed. I laughed too so they didn't know i was spying. (Actually, some of it was a bit funny.) Then Angela Carr (code name Grey

Wolf) said they ort to do a poster about it and i said that was a good idea so they went to ask Desmond to do a picture for it. (Desmond hasn't got a code name because he isn't a proper Noodle. *Or an Anti-*Noodle.) *Anyway he done this picture of Graham (code name Leonardo) looking a bit like Kwasimodo. It was very good. You could tell who it was meant to be and we all had a good laugh. (Peter said he could use it on his cake, so there you are, fame at last!!!) Anyway they said how was we going to get everyone else to see the poster and i said the best thing is to get it photcopied and i said leave that to me. Which is what i done. We're putting the posters up round the school tomorrow but i thought youd like to see one first.*

Signing off. Rasputin.

Taped to the bottom of the report was the poster. Beneath the cartoon figure of Graham, it read:

Be afraid. Be very afraid. The Anti-Noodles are breaking free of their chains… Graham "Bloodaxe" Keefe IS Caliban in *The Tempest*. Come and marvel! Come and tremble! March 4th to 6th – your date with DESTINY!

Nathan puffed out his cheeks and tapped the poster, but it was clear that he didn't know what to say. He was running out of encouraging comments.

"They've really got it in for me, haven't they?" said Graham. "What do you think I should do?"

"You could ignore it."

"That won't be easy. Not if they put these up all over the place, and not if I appear as a cake design."

"I suppose not."

"And it's not going to do our election chances much good, either."

"Still, she has given you a bit of warning, hasn't she?"

"She also got the damn things photocopied for them. Which is a bit *active* for a spy, when you come to think about it."

Graham hesitated and looked at Nathan.

"She came round here again last night," he said.

"Did she? What for?"

"She thought there was a meeting. I smuggled her out before anyone noticed, but I can't be doing with this, Nathan. It's going to look weird, her pottering about in Dad's shed as if she owns it."

"She has got a knack for getting things wrong, hasn't she?"

"Maybe. I think she might've got this wrong on purpose."

"Why should she do that?"

"I don't know but I reckon I'm going to have to tell her to clear off. I mean, I've tried to be nice about it but she doesn't take any notice. I'm going to have to make it very plain..."

"Hmm," said Nathan, frowning to himself and taking a drink from his can. "Unless..."

"Unless what?"

"Well, maybe she keeps coming round because there's nowhere else for her to go."

"She could just stay at home, couldn't she?" Graham said.

He screwed the poster into a tight ball and lobbed it into the bin.

"Well, I don't know, Graham. That's what I was thinking about. Maybe she doesn't *like* to stay at home. I mean, with her dad being in Africa or wherever he is..."

"Not in Africa, Nathan. I don't believe that."

"All right, then, he's not in Africa. But it could be there's *something* she doesn't want to stay home for."

"Oh, yes. She'd rather be in some mucky old shed than her own home."

"It's possible. It could be that your shed is *nicer* than her place."

Graham stared at him. Because Nathan was so slow in everything he did and said, you could be fooled into thinking he was a person without ideas; but, on certain occasions, he could see things that other people missed. Graham wondered whether this was one of those occasions.

"You mean," he said slowly, "it's a sort of *refuge*?"

"Could be. She comes round to your shed to get some peace and quiet."

"Because," said Graham. "Because..."

He paused. He could see her now, a little round scene-shifter, her face bright and purposeful, galumphing pointlessly round the hall and getting in the way of the actors.

"Because he gives her a bad time," Nathan said. "Who knows?"

"My God. She's afraid of him."

"We don't know that. It's only a theory, Graham. It *could* be that he belts her. That happens. It could be that I'm totally wrong."

Graham traced a finger over the pattern in the tablecloth and said nothing for a while. He was recalling all those times when Beth had latched on to him. Pretending she knew his name. Turning up in the sandwich room. And then the shed. And all those mad stories about gorillas... And *why* did she latch on to him? Because he didn't send her away with a flea in her ear. He remembered with something of a pang that he'd tried to, but first Vicki had stopped him, and now here was Nathan with this new theory, giving him further pause for thought.

"I wonder if she pestered anyone else," he said eventually. "Before she got to us, I mean."

"I wouldn't be surprised. She's a pestering sort of person."

"But they had no time for her, so she's ended up with us."

"That's what I was thinking," said Nathan ponderously. "But I reckon there's another reason, too."

"What?"

"Well, your dad doesn't get in till after seven, does he? And your mum works late at the library, and Toby's always with that Barry kid..."

"So?"

"So the house is more or less empty for a couple of hours after school. No one around asking awkward questions."

"Yes, you're right."

Graham felt suddenly disconcerted. The thought that Beth had somehow tricked him was an odd, slightly uncomfortable one. She'd always seemed too straightforward and simple to be capable of tricking anyone, like a guileless little dog. And yet she had tricked him. But he also felt rather relieved, too. She was interested in the house, not him, and that was easier to deal with.

"Maybe we should give her another chance," he said. "What do you think?"

"Yes, I think we should. I think we should at least be sure. After all, if she's, you know..."

"Poor kid."

They sat thinking their own thoughts until they heard feet scuffling outside the back door. Graham looked at his watch.

"Mum and Toby," he said. "They're back early."

In an hour or so Dad would be back too. He'd come cycling down the path, whistling softly to himself, and maybe he'd bring the evening paper in. He'd show Graham the cricket scores from Australia and they'd pore over them together, talking about who'd done well and what the prospects for tomorrow were and whether it was wise to go into the match without a spinner.

"It makes you grateful for what you've got, doesn't it?" he said to Nathan. "I mean, Toby can be a pain in the buttocks but he is my brother and he's no bother really."

"Yeah. Toby's all right."

"And then there's Mum. Good old Mum..."

"Yeah."

"And Dad, of course. You can *trust* Dad. It kind of counts for something, doesn't it?"

Nathan lowered his eyes and studied his spread hands.

"God, Nathan, I'm sorry. I only meant..."

"That's OK. Your dad's OK."

"I wasn't thinking. I never think..."

"It doesn't matter," Nathan said. "Just because my dad cleared off ..."

"Oh God, I'm sorry..."

"... and Beth's dad might be no good, it doesn't mean the whole tribe of dads is no good. And my dad didn't knock me about, did he? He never did. So that's OK, Graham. I take your point."

He smiled and that made Graham feel even more wretched.

"Yes, but I ought to *think* more," he said. "I've got to think of other people..."

There was a tap at the window and they turned round to see Beth's face pressed against the glass.

"Good grief," said Graham, jumping up. "She's back *again*!"

INTRUDERS

Dad picked his way across the living-room floor, treading carefully in the gaps left by Toby's cars. He found a space and balanced in it on one foot, then the other, as he removed his cycle clips.

"Been in the shed, have you, Toby?" he asked, and Graham looked up from his book.

There were no signs in the shed, surely. He and Nathan had hustled Beth out of the house and round the corner to the chip shop. They'd been kind and sympathetic – they hadn't nagged her or made her feel unwanted – and they'd checked the shed thoroughly, so there couldn't have been any signs, could there?

Toby brought a small sports car to a screeching halt by Dad's boot.

"Toby?"

"What?"

"Not what. Pardon."

"Eh?"

"Don't say what, say pardon."

"Oh."

He backed the car and manoeuvred it in the direction of a Jeep lurking behind one of his trainers.

"Toby!"

"What?"

"Have you been in the shed?"

"Yes. Why?"

"Have you moved things around in there? Some time this week?"

"I haven't been in there this week."

"I thought you said..."

"What is it, Dad?" Graham asked casually.

"What?"

"What's wrong with the shed?"

"Oh, nothing," Dad said, falling into the armchair and easing his boots off. "Nothing really. Things have been tidied, that's all. Things in pots..."

The daisies, Graham thought. The daisies in the flowerpots. I checked the floor but I didn't check the shelves.

"It might've been me," he said.

"Really? Things in pots..."

"Yes. That sounds like me..."

"What's it in aid of, then?"

"It's an experiment," Graham said after a moment's hesitation. "Science. To do with light and things."

"Ah. I wondered."

"You want me to put things back the way they were?"

"No, no. It doesn't matter. I just, you know, wondered."

Graham wondered too. He wondered whether to say anything more. It was Beth, actually. This little kid from school. And she was in our shed because of her dad – possibly – we're not sure but we think ... well...

No. Too many awkward questions to be faced. Let it slide.

But he knew he couldn't let it slide for ever. He'd have to do something or Beth would come trolling round again. And, if Nathan's theory was right, he couldn't simply tell her to clear off. *If* Nathan was right...

I'll have to find out, he thought. I'll have to know about how things are at home for Beth. Just in case. I don't want to be too hard on her. Not without reason. I'll find out first.

He returned to his book, gazing at the words without reading them. Behind his eyes he was trying to think of ways to visit Beth's home – without Beth being there; without Amanda being there either. Especially without Amanda being there. He recalled his last encounter with Amanda and could quite easily imagine a brutal streak there somewhere. The Rayburn brutal streak. Handed down from father to daughter, probably.

"Well, I warned you," Dad muttered from the armchair. "I said you'd run into trouble."

"Yes, but what else can I do?" said Graham at once.

Dad gave him a puzzled look over the top of the evening paper.

"What?" he asked.

"Nothing," said Graham. "I thought you said something..."

"I did, Graham. I said I warned them. I said there'd be trouble if they went into the test without a spinner."

He folded the paper and lobbed it at Graham.

"Take a look at those scores and you'll see what I mean."

It wasn't difficult to find out Beth's address. Nathan saw her in the sandwich room and asked her to write it in Graham's notebook.

"Why?"

"Why? Well, we need it for our records. The Anti-Noodles records," Nathan explained awkwardly. "You know, the database..."

He thought it sounded feeble – a database with only four people in it – but Beth seemed satisfied and happily wrote it down for him.

"It's a bit of a scribble," she said as she pushed the book back at him. "But I had to be quick. We don't want the Noodles to see us talking, do we?"

"No," said Nathan. "That's a good point."

He cast his eyes round the room. They were the only two there, apart from Mr Trainor, who was asleep at the front.

"I didn't put my proper name either," she whispered, gathering up her sandwiches and moving to a seat at the back. "I put Rasputin. In case the book gets into the wrong hands. They won't know it's me then, see."

"Unless they already know where you live."

"Oh, yes. Maybe I should put a false address..."

"Then *we* wouldn't know where you live."

"That's true. Anyway, I don't think they will. Not many people do. We've only been here a little while, you see, and..."

She stopped. Her eyes grew wide and she held up a finger.

"Someone's coming."

They watched the door but no one came.

"Beth?" Nathan said after a while.

He turned to look at her. She was gazing out of the window, chewing steadily and showing no signs of having heard.

"One more thing, Beth. We ought to have a chat about moving this scenery. Make a few plans and stuff."

No answer. Nathan checked the rest of the room. They were still completely alone.

"You doing anything after school?" he said.

Still no answer.

"Only, perhaps we could talk about it then."

She got up, stuffed the remains of her lunch in her bag and made for the door. As she passed Nathan, she slid the corner of a paper bag onto his desk. There was a message scrawled on it in biro.

Hall, it said. *Harf past three. R.*

While Nathan kept Beth busy in the hall, Graham slung his bag over his shoulder, pulled his collar up and made his way out of the school gates. When he reached the street he looked nervously from side to side before turning right and heading towards Beth's house. It was a bad time to attempt such a furtive mission. The Noodles' posters had appeared dotted around the school earlier that day, and he'd been the subject of public curiosity ever since. People pointed him out to each other, whispering behind their hands. Look, there goes Bloodaxe, the one on the poster. What's he up to now? Where's he going?

No, a bad time to be attempting anything secretively. But that couldn't be helped. He had to know the secret of Beth's background. He wasn't exactly sure what he was going to do when he found the house. He had a vague feeling that he'd walk by and glance in at a lighted window. And Beth's father would be there. Crop-haired, swigging from a bottle. Track-suit bottoms and a vest. Lunging at the dog with his boot, and the dog yelping and cowering behind the sofa.

Of course, it would have to be a pretty big window to see all that. And the picture might be very different anyway. He might be a mild-mannered man with thinning hair and glasses. He might be sitting at the table doing a jigsaw, with Beth's mum, her hand on his shoulder, smiling fondly down at him. Nathan might be entirely wrong about all this.

But that was the point of going. To find out.

The streets on Beth's estate were all named after trees, which struck Graham as ironic because the only trees he could see were spindly specimens caged behind stakes and wire. There were also clumps of grey bushes hiding crisp packets and bent cans, and patches of dull, scrubby grass criss-crossed with trodden paths. He walked slowly down Larch Close, looking at house numbers out of the corner of his eye. Someone was sitting on a front step mending a puncture. With a start Graham saw that it was George Marriott. He quickened his pace and nipped across the street.

"Watch where you're going, you fool!"

A broad woman on a small moped braked to avoid him. She slowed to a stop and planted two large feet on the road. Graham cringed like a rabbit and dropped his bag. Snatching it up, he darted behind a phone box on the other side of the street. He peered at her through the glass and for a moment thought she was going to come for him. She wore a puffy cream-grey jacket and a helmet that looked as if it had been dredged from the mud of a First World War trench. Her face was contorted beneath its chin-strap. She looked like someone who elbowed lorries aside in heavy traffic.

Oh God, thought Graham, I'm going to get beaten up by an old lady before I even find the blessed house.

He saw George come to his gate to see what was going on, his greasy hands held out before him like a surgeon.

And a Noodle as a witness, Graham thought.

But the woman merely shouted at him again and putt-putted off. George watched her go and then went back to his puncture. He looked oddly normal out of school. Busy with his bike and sensible.

Graham sighed with relief and continued gingerly up the street. He found Beth's house – number 35 – at the end of a run of four. It was neat and quiet and probably empty. He walked slowly by, taking in as much as he could without staring straight at it. He saw nothing unusual. Ordinary curtains and the back of an ordinary sofa; tidy-ish shrubs in the front garden; some stickers in an upstairs window. No clues about the people who lived there. He turned and walked slowly back again. From the front it certainly looked as if they were out.

All this way, he thought, risking all manner of danger, and I've learned not a thing.

So, making sure the street was empty, he pushed open the gate and went into the garden. He did it before he had the time to reason himself out of it. Through the front window he saw what he might expect to see in any room: a TV, a sideboard, the sofa, a few papers on a low table. Then he went stealthily to the side of the house and edged into a narrow passageway. At the end he could see a triangle of lawn and part of a border of flowers. Before he was halfway down the passage, he changed his mind and turned round.

This is daft, he told himself. What am I likely to find out like this, anyway? They're out. There's no one here.

Unless they're being *deliberately* quiet, he thought suddenly.

Maybe Beth's dad *was* there, pressed against the wall, a broken chair leg in his hand, waiting for Graham to pop his head round the corner. Or on his knees, feeding raw meat to a Doberman. Looking up and scowling as Graham appeared...

Just then he heard the chugging of a small engine in the street and he froze in his tracks.

The engine cut out and the front gate squeaked open.

The garden, he thought. Go for the garden. Jump over a fence. Go, go, go! No. Think of the chair leg. Or the dog. No, keep low and dive for the gate before they know you're here. Surprise them. Move, Graham! Now!

But he stood there, unable to move either forward or back, and a broad figure appeared at the far end of the passageway. It filled the gap and struggled with the handlebars of a moped, like a cowboy wrestling a steer. The figure saw him and stopped.

"What the—" it said. "You again!"

"Oh, hello," Graham began with feeble good cheer.

She came at him with her helmet lowered. His blood ran cold and his knees shook.

"What the hell are you doing in my garden?" she asked.

"Your garden?"

It was Beth's mum. The woman who'd almost run him over ten minutes ago was Beth's mum.

"'Course it's my garden. What did you think?"

"Yes," he said. "I – I thought it was..."

"First you fling yourself under my wheels and then I find you snooping round my property. I think you'd better explain yourself, young man."

She unstrapped her helmet and took it off. The change this made to her features was startling but also something of a relief. With the strap under her chin her face had been creased and angry. It had looked a bit like a balled-up sock. When the helmet came off a frizz of yellowish hair was released and her cheeks became smooth and somehow amiable. She widened her eyes and stretched her jaws. For a second Graham thought she was going to scream at him, but she was only loosening the tension in her face muscles.

"Well?" she said, leaning behind her to take a shopping bag from the box on the back of the moped. "What're you up to?"

"I – I was looking for you," Graham stammered.

"Looking for me? Why?"

"To say sorry. For jumping out at you like that."

"I should think so. Mad thing to do."

She handed him the shopping and nodded down the passageway.

"Go on," she said. "Back door."

"I'd better be getting off, actually."

"Back door, now!"

Graham took the shopping meekly to the back door and waited for her.

"It's not locked. In you go."

In the kitchen the lights flickered on and he saw blue cupboard doors and a pile of plates and saucepans on a draining-board. A funny little table made out of cardboard tubes and a stack of round flat tins stood in one corner. There was something crude and child-like about it, and something familiar about those tins… Mrs Rayburn banged the door and cut across his thoughts.

"Though maybe it *should've* been locked," she said darkly. "With snoopers about."

"I wasn't snooping, honestly. I was – I was…"

"Looking for me."

"Yes."

"Even though you saw me driving off up the street?"

"Well, yes. But I was going to leave a note…"

"Oh yes?"

"Or tell someone else. Your husband. Say sorry to him."

She filled the kettle and switched it on. Then she turned and leaned against the sink with her arms folded.

"My husband?"

"In case he was in, yes."

"And he wasn't."

"No."

"He wouldn't be. How did you know where I lived?"

"Where you lived?"

"Here. Where I live. How did you know?"

"Oh, yes. Well, George told me."

"I don't know any George."

"The boy mending his bike. That's George. He knows you."

She continued staring at him while the kettle began to purr.

"So George told you, did he?" she said eventually. "And what possessed you to jump in the road like that?"

He gave a little laugh which faded away in a whimper.

"I didn't know what I was doing," he said. "I haven't been very well, actually."

"What's been wrong with you?"

"I've had this sort of fever. Been running a temperature. Sometimes I don't know what I'm doing. I was walking along and I thought I saw this dog and I just had to get out of its way..."

"So you jumped in the path of a speeding moped?"

"Yes. Though I didn't know it was a moped. All I could see was this dog with dripping jaws..."

"Sounds like you should've been in bed."

"Yes, I should."

"You live round here? I've never seen you before."

"No. I live the other side. Near the Common."

"By the prison?"

"Yes."

"So what are you doing over here?"

"I'm not sure, Mrs Rayburn. I sort of came out of school in a daze and I ended up here. Do you think I could sit down?"

"I think you'd better."

She watched him wipe his brow and lower himself carefully onto a kitchen stool. He sat clutching his bag and looking at the floor.

"I think I'd better call your mother, too," she said. "What's your number?"

"Number?"

"Phone number."

He swallowed.

"It's er ... 35 ... 35..."

"3535? Is that all?"

"No. 35 ... Or 53 ... I know it but it's kind of slipped my mind..."

"Really? Has it? Then I'll have to look it up, won't I? What's your name? Or has that slipped your mind as well?"

"No, no," he said, trying to force his mind into another gear.

It wouldn't go. He couldn't think of a name to give her.

This is the end of the line, he thought. She's got me now. I can do no more.

"It's Graham," he said. "Graham Keefe."

"Graham Keefe?"

He thought she'd recognize it – Beth was sure to have mentioned him – but she didn't.

"Right, Graham. Wait there."

She picked up a wall phone, wedging it between her ear and her shoulder while she flicked through the directory. As she dialled he remembered that they were still in that dead time, the time he usually disliked, when Mum was at work and Toby at his friend's house. He offered a silent prayer of thanks for working mothers and little brothers with friends.

"Out," said Mrs Rayburn, replacing the phone. "Some people. A sick child and they go gallivanting out."

"She'll be in bed," said Graham. "She's not very well either."

"What's the matter with her?"

"Same as me. She caught it from me, in fact..."

"Well, I'm not sending you off in that state, young man. Mandy'll be in in a minute. She can see you home."

"Thank you. Thank you very much..."

Then he thought, Mandy? She means Amanda. Who'll tell her everything. And then kill me.

He jumped up so quickly that the stool rocked.

"I'll be all right," he said, trying to steady it.

He grabbed his bag and sent a pile of letters fluttering off the table.

"It comes and goes," he explained. "And it's gone now. I feel much better actually."

"You don't look it."

"But I am, honestly. I've got about half an hour before it strikes again, and I can be home in twenty minutes..."

He stooped to pick up the letters. Two brown with windows and a white one, neatly typed with the name of some firm or other in the top left corner. Mr D. G. Rayburn, 35, Larch Close: Beth's dad. The initials made it seem respectable. As if someone called Mr D. G. Rayburn couldn't possibly be violent. He handed the letters to Beth's mother and backed towards the door. She took them and was about to say something when they both heard the sound of a key in a lock.

"That'll be Mandy. If you just wait there a moment..."

She went into the hall so Graham took his chance and bolted.

When he got home Nathan was waiting for him.

"She's on her way," he said nervously.

"What?"

"Beth. She's on her way."

"I thought she was with you..."

"She was, but she said she'd better report back to you."

"So why isn't she with you now?"

"Because we came by different routes. She said she shouldn't be seen with me, in case we ran into any Noodles."

"Great," said Graham, sighing and slinging his bag in a corner.

Nathan dropped into a chair and asked tentatively, "So how did you get on?"

"Wonderful. I was almost run over by her mother, who then trapped me in her kitchen and started firing questions at me…"

"Did you tell her why you were there?"

"Of course not. But I told her my name. I had to. She kept on at me."

"What about her old man?"

"No sign. I put my life in danger and learned not a single thing, Nathan."

Then he remembered the letters he fumbled off the kitchen table.

"Except his name," he said. "Or his initials. D. G. They were on a letter. Which doesn't exactly tell us a lot."

"And nothing else?"

"No. Well, I saw where the letter was from," he added and closed his eyes to try to see it more clearly. "Yes, that's right. There was the name of some firm on it, too. Majestic something. Majestic Services."

"Never heard of them. What do they do?"

"If I knew I would've said…"

"Majestic, Majestic," Nathan muttered to himself. "Hey. Majestic. That's the cinema, isn't it?"

"What, the Complex?"

"Yes. Its proper name is the Majestic."

Of course it was. The Majestic Cinema. A few years ago, when it was re-opened after refurbishment, the manager announced in the paper that it was now "an entertainment complex". Which meant that there were two screens instead of one and a small room up a flight of stairs with a pool table in it – the Hot Pot Pool Club. The Hot Pot didn't operate any more – there'd been a fire and some row about money – but the "entertainment complex" name stuck.

"The cinema," mused Graham. "I wonder why they're writing to him."

"I don't know. Maybe he works there..."

"Maybe. We can't be sure."

"Well, did you see anything else while you were there?" Nathan asked.

Graham closed his eyes again and tried to summon up Mrs Rayburn's kitchen. He saw the sink and the blue cupboards and...

"Yes," he said. "There was something else. A sort of table made of old tins. A botched up thing it was. Looked as if Beth had made it. Out of these round, flat tins. I remember thinking I'd seen tins like that before..."

Nathan jumped in his chair and tried to snap his fingers.

"Round flat tins," he said. "Like they keep film in?"

"Of course! Which means he probably does work at the Complex. So if we snoop about and keep our eyes open..."

Then Beth was calling outside the back door.

"Coo-ee. It's me!"

They jumped up and rushed outside.

"No one saw me," she said. "We're quite safe."

"But not for long," Graham said, taking her elbow and guiding her down the garden. "Dad's noticed things moved about in the shed –"

"Ooops."

"– and he's not going to like it if his seed packets are stuck on the walls for pictures and—"

"But I don't do that, Graham," she said, disappointment clouding her face.

"Not yet, maybe, but—"

"And I need somewhere private. So I can write my reports and stuff."

"Yes," he said, "of course. If you really need to ... well, need to find somewhere, you can use the shed. I'm just saying, you know, be careful. You don't want to draw attention to yourself."

"Oh, that's all right, Graham," she said, breaking into one of her smiles. "You won't even know I'm here."

WILD MAN

So, most afternoons after school, Beth made her way to the shed and pottered about, and Graham and Nathan tried to ignore her. They sat in the kitchen and plotted their next move against the Noodles, or they talked about how they might get to see Mr Rayburn in his lair, somewhere at the cinema, though Nathan was less enthusiastic about this than Graham.

"What are we supposed to do?" he said one afternoon. "We can't just march in and ask to see him, can we?"

"No, we need a reason. If we can think of a message to take him or something, that might do it."

"Hmm."

"What do you mean, hmm?"

"What sort of message are we likely to have for someone who works at the cinema? They won't believe us."

"They will if the message is good enough. That's what we have to do – think up a really good message."

But that's what they couldn't do. Nothing they thought of sounded *real*, so, after a while, they took a break and went down to the shed to make sure that Beth hadn't taken it into her head to apply some paint or put up wallpaper. They found the door wedged shut.

"Perhaps she's gone," said Nathan. "Without saying anything."

"Not her. She *always* says something. Anyway, she can't've gone. The door would open if she had."

They rattled it and called her name. After a moment or two, they heard the clack of wood against wood, and something heavy being dragged out of the way. Then the door opened a crack and an eye appeared.

"Yes?" she said.

She peered at them as if they were salesmen with dodgy goods to sell.

"What's going on in there?" Graham asked.

"Nothing," she said. "I'm just being careful. You never know who might turn up."

"Yes you do. There's only us around."

"You'd better come in, then."

She stood aside to let them in. Her cheeks were streaked with dirt and sweat and her jeans were stiff with mud. She looked like a miniature commando and she was breathing hard. Graham looked suspiciously about him for signs that she had been "tidying up", but the only thing out of place was the wheelbarrow. It was usually outside, propped against the side of the shed.

"What's that doing in here?" he said, fixing her with a beady eye.

"It's not doing nothing. I moved it in because of the rain."

"What rain?"

"I thought it was about to rain. Then it would get rusty and—"

"No, Beth. Leave things as they are. I did tell you."

"I was just being helpful..."

"You *thought* you were being helpful, but you weren't. Is that why we couldn't get in?"

"Probably. I was just writing my report so I put it by the door," she said, adding imperiously, "I didn't want to be disturbed."

Nathan shuffled his feet a little and looked guilty.

"And why are you so filthy?" Graham continued. "How can anyone get filthy writing reports?"

"Very easily," she said, "if people have wheelbarrows what have wonky wheels and trip people up when they're moving 'em."

"Anyway," Nathan said, "you had something to report, did you?"

"Ah, well, I have, as it happens."

She pointed to an old tool box and a barrel and invited them to sit. Graham lowered himself reluctantly onto the barrel, then stood up again.

"There's mud all over this barrel," he said. "Look at my trousers."

"It's a shed, Graham," Beth told him with a sigh. "What did you expect? Cushions? Now, do you want to hear my report or not?"

"You'd better get on with it," Nathan said. "You'll have to go soon."

"Right. Pay attention, then."

In the gloom, excitement glinted briefly in her eyes.

"Rasputin's Report Number Four," she said and paused dramatically. "Guess what?"

"We can't guess," Graham said irritably. "Tell us."

"We've had an intruder!"

"What, here?"

"No."

"You mean the Noodles have had an intruder?" Nathan asked.

"No, no. At home. What do you make of that?"

Graham shifted uncomfortably on his barrel and said nothing.

"It happened last week but I only just found out about it. Mum didn't tell me because she didn't want to worry me. She does that sometimes. Keeps things from me. I found out from

Amanda. She didn't mind saying about it. She knows I can cope."

"Who was he?" Graham asked. "Or she. It might've been a she, I suppose."

"No, it was a *youth*," Beth said, making the word sound slightly disgusting. "One of these tearaways. Mum caught him red-handed snooping round by the back door, and she asked him what he was up to and who he was..."

"And who was he?"

"Well, Mum can't remember. He told her his name but he probably made it up so it doesn't really matter. They do that, some of them, give false names. He was real shifty. Mum said he was all pasty-faced and thin. Sort of ratty looking—"

"What did he want?" Graham interrupted, as casually as he could.

"To rob us, probably."

She leaned back and folded her arms proudly.

"What do you make of that?"

"Maybe he was just lost," Nathan said with a half-glance at Graham to see how he was taking all this.

"How could he get lost outside our back door?"

"Maybe he didn't know where he was. You know, sort of gormless, a bread roll short of a picnic..."

Graham got to his feet and, even though there was little room for it, began to pace about and wave his arms.

"This is all very fascinating," he said, "but it's nothing to do with the Noodles, is it? And that's what your reports are supposed to be about."

"I know, but all they do at the moment is yak on about the election and Peter Smith's blinking cake. They reckon it's going to get a whassname – a certificate – in the Display of Work. Even with Graham's face on it."

"What do you mean 'even'?" Graham said.

"Maybe the Anti-Noodles should enter something," suggested Nathan.

Beth slapped him across the shoulder.

"We are. Vicki is. She's putting in some handwriting. Different coloured inks and stuff..."

"Calligraphy," said Graham.

"No, just handwriting, I think. Actually, I could put something in myself. I'm quite good with my hands. I made this table once—"

"Is Vicki's handwriting going to be as good as Smith's cake, I wonder," Nathan interrupted. "It would be a bit rough if a Noodle got a certificate and we didn't. Maybe we should think of something else."

"Yes," said Beth, jumping up. "Good point. I know what we'll do. We'll scrag them!"

"What?"

"Move in fast and scrag them. An ambush."

Nathan looked doubtful and held up a finger.

"What exactly do you mean by scragging?" he asked.

"Jump on them when they're not expecting it."

"Hang on," said Graham. "We were talking about the Display of Work. And, anyway, the Anti-Noodles is a non-violent organization..."

"We don't have to beat them up –"

Beat them up? Nathan and Beth, *beating up* Noodles?

"– but we could grab their hats and chuck them away. That kind of thing."

"That's still fairly violent..."

"We could be in and out before they knew what was going on."

"And they'd know it was us."

"They don't wear hats, do they?" said Nathan.

"No, forget the violence," Graham added quickly. "Besides, you can't have an ambush with only two."

"Three," said Beth. "There's three of us."

"*You* can't scrag people! You're too short. And anyway you're supposed to be a spy."

"I could throw off my disguise at the last moment. And as a matter of fact, there's Vicki. That makes four."

"I don't think Vicki should be involved in scragging people," Nathan said. "She's a girl..."

"So am I!"

"Yes, but not like Vicki..."

"I am! In fact, I'd be good at it because they wouldn't be expecting me to turn on them."

"Look," said Graham, "calm down, Beth. You could get us all into deep trouble here."

Yet again she was steering things down the wrong path and Graham sensed that, if he didn't take control, she'd drag them after her. All this talk of jumping on people and throwing imaginary hats all over the place. He could foresee arms twisted behind backs and knees in groins. He recalled Angela Carr thumping him in the face with her PE bag, back in his primary school days; the water welling up in his eyes and the tingling at the back of his nose. He didn't want to provoke that kind of thing again.

"Listen," he said. "We'll do something about the Noodles, I promise. Meanwhile, don't go charging into them like some pit bull first thing tomorrow morning."

"OK, Graham. I'll wait till we've made the plan."

They made her repeat her promise twice – no scragging – and she nodded fiercely. But Graham knew they'd have to watch her carefully over the next couple of days. It was all too easy to picture her flinging off her disguise and biting Noodles in the ankle.

For much of that evening Graham sat in his room under a pool of light from the lamp on his desk, doodling ideas about the Noodles on scraps of paper but thinking mostly about Beth's father.

What if he's not the thug we think he is? he found himself wondering. Suppose he's just an ordinary dad. If we go sticking our noses into a normal family life, we could be making a huge mistake. A huge, *embarrassing* mistake. On the other hand, if he *is* a thug, if Beth *does* need to keep out of his way ... well, we *have* to stick our noses in, don't we? We have to do something.

He lobbed his scribblings into the basket and went to phone Nathan.

"Made any progress?" he asked.

"With what?"

Sometimes Nathan's lack of urgency made Graham feel quite lonely.

"With getting to see Beth's old man. What do you think?"

"Ah, that. Well, no. Not yet. Have you?"

"Sort of. I'll fill in the details tomorrow. And I think we should tell Beth there'll be a meeting on Friday."

"On Friday. Right. What for?"

"To talk about the Noodles. I reckon the

prospect of a meeting might keep her at bay for a day or so. And it'll give us the chance to call at the Complex on Thursday."

The line went quiet for a moment.

"Nathan?"

"Yes?"

"You're still there, then? You're still with me?"

"Yes. The Complex on Thursday. What's on?"

"I don't know! We're not going to see what's on. We're going to see Beth's dad."

"Ah! I get it now. You're sure this is wise, are you, Graham? We don't know what he's like and—"

"It's because we don't know what he's like that we have to go."

"Right. I see. What are we going to say to him, then?"

"I'll tell you tomorrow morning."

He caught up with Nathan just before the next lunch-time rehearsal in the hall, sidled up to him and whispered a few curt instructions out of the side of his mouth.

"Thursday. Four o'clock."

"What?"

"We go in and ask to see him..."

"Eh?"

"Beth's dad. Thursday, at the Complex."

"Oh, that."

"Of course," Graham said. "That."

"I'm not so sure this is going to work, you know," Nathan said.

"What?"

"This going to the Complex."

"It'll be all right, Nathan. I've worked it out. We'll say we're doing a project, see. And we've written to Mr Rayburn and he said he'd help us."

"But they might check with school and—"

"They won't. They won't be bothered. And anyway, we'll be using false names."

"False names?"

"Yes. I'll be William Baker and you'll be Julian Clements."

"Why do I have to be Julian? Can't I be something else?"

"Be what you like, only make sure you let me know."

"Right. Henry, then. Henry Baker."

"No. I'm William Baker and you're…"

"Henry Clements. Yes. Got it."

"We go in. Wave a letter at them and ask to see Beth's dad. He's written to us, see. And we've come to talk about working in a cinema…"

"Doing what?"

"I don't know. It doesn't matter."

"But maybe what he does has nothing to do with films. Maybe he cleans the toilets or something. Maybe he runs the Hot Pot…"

"The Pool Club? That's closed down."

"But maybe they'll open it up again or..."

"Then we talk about entertainment in general..."

"But he'll know he hasn't written to us."

"We don't tell *him* he's written to us, Nathan. Obviously. We just ask him a few questions about whatever he does, and we take notes and size him up."

"Do you reckon we'll be able to tell what he's like just by asking him about playing snooker or cleaning out toilets?"

"He doesn't clean out toilets. That's only what you said. And yes, I think we'll be able to tell *something*."

"I'm not so sure, Graham."

"Look, if you've got a better idea, let's hear it."

"No, no, I haven't."

"Thursday at four it is, then."

"OK," said Nathan unhappily. "But you do the talking. Henry Baker, right?"

"No. I'm Henry Baker. You're Julian Williams. No, wait a minute. You're Julian Clements and I'm ... look, I'll write the names down. You'll have a couple of days to learn who you're supposed to be."

"Right. And where's this letter coming from that we wave about. I mean, if he *hasn't* actually written to us..."

"No! We write it. It's simple enough, for

heaven's sake..."

At this point Mrs Backhouse called everyone together and Graham turned his attention reluctantly to the rehearsal. He wasn't happy about leaving Nathan in such a state of confusion, but his unease didn't last long. He found, slightly to his surprise, that he was looking forward to being Caliban for a while. The last time they'd rehearsed, he'd scuttled about at the feet of Prospero, leering at him and mouthing insults. There was something liberating about this, especially as Prospero was Anthony Dawkins, a tall, rather superior individual who had laughed hysterically at Graham's football shorts earlier in the year.

"A south-west blow on ye and blister you all o'er!" he'd rasped at Dawkins, the day of the shorts firmly in his mind. "All the charms of Sycorax, toads, beetles, bats, light on you!"

And Mrs Backhouse had been impressed.

"Yes, Graham," she'd said. "Lovely *venom* there! Keep it up!"

Today, however, she was telling them they would not be rehearsing the text.

"We need to go over some of the technical stuff," she said, her fingers knotted as if she were praying. "Talk a bit about lighting and sound; how the play is going to *look*. And I'm going to run through some of the duties of the stage crew."

She gestured at Beth, Vicki and Nathan.

Beth, with a look of profound pleasure on her face, shot her hand up.

"In a minute, Beth," said Mrs Backhouse, very calmly. "The rest of you may have noticed that the costumes are ready. I'd like you to try them on and get used to them."

She waved an arm airily at a table in the corner.

"They've all been set out over there. And they're all labelled. I've set aside two rooms across the corridor for you to change in. Girls, in LC 4 and boys, LC 6. We haven't much time, so get into them quickly and let's have a look at you. A parade round the hall in six minutes, OK?"

There was an outbreak of chattering and a general surge towards the costumes. Graham was about to join in when she called him to one side.

"How are you feeling about Caliban, Graham?" she asked quietly.

"Fine," he said. "I think I'm getting to grips with it."

"I think so, too. In fact, I think you've done extremely well. I'm very pleased with the way you've tackled such a *challenging* part."

Graham smiled and tried to look modest.

"Of course," she added, "you have to remember, when you're on stage you're *not* you. You're Caliban."

"Yes," he said. "I know."

"A wild man. In some ways a rather *gruesome* character. People will react to that. Audiences are sometimes *repelled* by him, and sometimes they laugh at him. Which is only right and proper. But, of course, they will be reacting not to Graham Keefe, but to Caliban."

"I see," he said, not quite sure what she was getting at but sensing, all the same, that he was being prepared for something unpleasant.

"You'll remember that, I'm sure," she said with a confidential smile.

When he got to the table he saw exactly what she meant. Most of the other costumes had been snatched away by this time, and it was all too obvious which was Caliban's. It was made up of a coil of dried leaves, a rope belt and a scrap of material that looked as if it had been used to mop up the canteen floor. The sight of it chilled Graham to his very heart.

He would be practically naked. He would have to prance around on stage in the less-than-semi-*nude*.

He turned in a panic to look for Mrs Backhouse but she was deep in conversation with the rest of the Anti-Noodles and pointing things out on a chart.

Graham found a corner in LC 6 and spread the skimpy costume on a desk. Then he looked round at the others. He was grateful that none of them paid him much attention. They were struggling into bulky tunics and vast cloaks, and seemed to be having a pretty good time of it. He undid his shirt, button by button, as slowly as he could. He folded it carefully, shook it out again, refolded it, turned his attention to his shoes. By the time he'd divested himself of most of his clothes, he was alone in the room and able to speed up. Crouching below the level of the desks, he wriggled out of his pants and slipped into the handful of rags Caliban was supposed to wear.

He stood up cautiously. And listened. Silence.

He padded towards the door, caught sight of himself in the glass, and stood there, stock still, for a second or two. It was worse than he'd imagined. He looked like a cross between Big Bird and a stripper.

Diving back to his pile of clothes, he hopped and wriggled until his pants were back on, then put the costume on top. He'd just finished when the door opened and Nathan looked in.

"Are you ready yet, because –"

The message dried in Nathan's throat.

"What?" said Graham, folding his arms and trying to look unconcerned. "What is it?"

"– because Mrs Backhouse wants to... Good grief, Graham, is that it?"

"You think I'd dress up like this for choice?"

"Are you sure you've got it all. I mean..."

"I'm wearing what I was given. The lot. OK? Any comments? Because if you have you can give them to your little friend out there."

"My little friend?"

"Beth. This is her fault. I wouldn't be here if she hadn't pushed me forward."

"Well, maybe, but you'd better get over to the hall. They're waiting for you."

"Right. See if anyone's coming, will you?"

Nathan leaned backwards into the corridor and looked both ways.

"All clear," he said. "Er ... are you..."

"What?"

"You've still got your socks on. I wondered whether you were supposed to..."

"I'm not walking down that corridor in bare feet."

"But, I mean, would Caliban wear socks, Graham?"

"And would he have to walk down a corridor where I know for a fact that a kid was sick last term? I think not, so make way, please."

"Right. Good point," said Nathan and he edged out of the room, still backwards.

Graham nipped over to the door and looked out for himself. Nathan was disappearing in the distance and there was no one else about. The door into the hall was about thirty paces away to his left. He fixed his eyes on it and then sprinted. He hit the door with such force that it burst open and he found himself skidding across the hall floor like a skater. He dug in his heels, trying desperately to stop the slide, but his socks had no grip so he glided on into the hall. A blur of people sidestepped out of his way. Then he clutched an elbow and swivelled to a halt.

The elbow belonged to Mrs Backhouse. She wrenched herself free and turned, about to snap at him. She did not snap but stood looking as if she'd been struck on the temple with a thick branch. In fact, Graham was aware of a dozen conversations petering out all around him. For a second or two he felt himself to be at the hub of a vast but silent wheel.

"Ah," said Mrs Backhouse eventually, "Caliban. Good ... *good*..."

She put her hands on her hips and stared at him from top to toe.

"Yes, good. Very *wild*. Although not exactly what I had in mind ... I can't quite put my finger on it," she said, and somebody sniggered.

Graham's face was burning. He kept his head down but, out of the corner of his eye, he caught sight of Beth waving her arm in the air.

"It's his pants, miss, I think," she offered. "If you look, his pants is bigger than his costume –"

Another outbreak of sniggering.

"– and they're stripy, miss. Like they've

come from M&S. I don't think they had M&S on this island, did they?"

"No," said Mrs Backhouse. "Well, perhaps we need to *rethink* Caliban's costume anyway. Stop that, the rest of you! It's not funny. This is theatre. You must learn to accept things for what they are *intended* to be, not for ... well, not for what they actually ... look like."

She glared round the group until the laughter died. Then she said quietly to Graham, "Sorry about this, Graham. I think we've miscalculated. Perhaps you'd better pop back and change now. And don't worry, we'll fill it out a little before the performance. OK?"

Graham didn't answer. He made for the hall door with as much dignity as he could muster. When he reached the corridor he leaned his back against the door and let the air hiss slowly through his nostrils.

That kid. That pesky little kid...

He strode angrily towards LR 6 and almost ran into Peter Smith and Angela Carr. They saw him and stopped. For a moment they were face to face. Graham waited, seething, for their laughter to shatter the silence but it did not come. They merely stared at him, too stunned to make a sound.

THE COMPLEX

It was the dead time again, when Mum and Toby were still out and Beth was pottering about in the shed by herself. Nathan was looking for something to eat and Graham was standing at the kitchen window staring down the garden.

"It was the silence I couldn't stand," he said. "The way they just looked at me."

"Shock, I expect," said Nathan, sawing wedge-shaped slices slowly from a loaf.

"It might've been better if they *had* laughed. I'll tell you what, though, Nathan. They won't leave it at that. We'll hear more from the Noodles about this before the week's out."

"Probably. Here, eat this."

Graham glanced at the plate which had been set next to him on the draining board. On it was a lump of bread the size and shape of a broken brick.

"What's this?"

"Peanut butter," said Nathan. "I know – it's not very neat. I can't cut bread neat. It's just one of the things I can't do."

Stretching his mouth to force it in, Graham continued to stare down the garden. Beth emerged carrying a bucket and tottered round the side of the shed with it.

"What the hell is she up to now?" Nathan asked.

"God knows," mumbled Graham through a mess of bread. "You know, I really ought to bawl her out about this."

"The bucket?"

"No, of course not the bucket. Who cares about a bucket?"

"Ah. You mean pointing out your pants like that..."

"Before the *whole* cast. And getting me into the play in the first place. She ought to be told."

"Why don't you tell her, then?"

"Because she wouldn't understand. She doesn't know what she's doing half the time. And, anyway, I don't want to think about it. The less said about it the better."

"Well, I'm not saying anything," Nathan said. "But others might."

"Quite. The Noodles. They'll love all this. It's practically handing them the election on a plate."

Graham looked down at his own plate and pushed some crumbs around with his finger.

"Nathan," he said after a while. "I don't think we should just give up on this election."

"Of course not."

"I think we should hold a rally of our own."

Nathan swivelled his eyes at him for a second, his jaw stilled, then looked down the garden again.

"You're sure?" he said and carried on eating.

"Yes. Why not?"

"It's just that lately things have a habit of, well, going wrong. Maybe we'd be better off doing something for the Display of Work..."

"No. It's got to be more public than that," Graham went on. "So. Friday lunch-time. In Yard Two. A mass meeting."

"All three of us, you mean."

"No, no. It'll be an event. People will come. I'm sure they will."

"That's what I'm afraid of," Nathan said, but only to himself.

"That's settled, then. Come on. Let's go and tell Beth."

Nathan touched his elbow.

"Beth?" he said. "Is that wise?"

"In case she tells the Noodles, you mean? I don't think we should be worried about them," Graham said, and he gave Nathan an enigmatic smile, a twitch at one corner of his lips.

They found the shed empty and, much to their relief, tidy. In fact, it looked unnaturally clean. Beth had obviously been working hard. She'd swept the floor so thoroughly that she'd cleared out the dirt from the cracks between the chipboard panels, and you could now see the brass screw-heads glinting at each corner.

"Gone," said Nathan. "She must've realized the time."

"Gone but not forgotten."

"It's kind of sad, Graham, don't you think?"

"What?"

"The way she's tidied up. Like she's making it into a home."

Graham nodded thoughtfully.

"She'll have carpet down if we don't watch her," he said. "The sooner we can get to see her dad the better. Clear this whole thing up."

"I don't know about clear it up. I mean, *if* we find him, and *if* we can prove he's being cruel ... well, we just know about it, don't we? We haven't exactly cleared it up."

"Maybe not," said Graham, "but we have to start somewhere, and that somewhere is the Complex. Tomorrow."

In spite of everything else that was occupying his mind, Graham couldn't stop worrying about his role as the half-naked Caliban. He feared that Smith would find some way of using it against him. Most of Thursday morning he was on edge. He went round corners in a state of nervous expectation, fearing a Noodle onslaught at any moment. Nothing happened – he hardly saw a Noodle all day, and when he did they ignored him – but the waiting left him tense and nervy.

"You look washed out," Nathan told him when they met outside the gates at the end of the day.

"I am. I've just had six and a half hours of looking over my shoulder."

"What for?"

"Noodles. They've been too quiet. They're not just working on Smith's cake, I bet."

"No, probably not," mused Nathan as they set off for the High Street. "They're probably going to strike some time soon. Maybe when the Display of Work opens, which is tomorrow, isn't it?"

"It is. Same time as the rally."

"Oh, I get it. We hold a rally so people don't go to see his prize-winning cake."

"Exactly. The more we can persuade to see us, the better," said Graham shrewdly.

Both screens were already showing films when they reached the Complex so there were no queues. They looked up and down the street a couple of times and then ambled into the foyer. A woman with blue tints in her hair and ornate glasses sat knitting behind a bank of sweets and popcorn. She was the woman who had mistaken them for Noodles and threatened to contact the school. There was no one else about, though, so they'd have to risk it.

"You did the letter?" Nathan asked.

Graham nodded. His mouth was dry and his hands sticky.

"Typed it out last night," he said.

He pulled it out of his pocket and looked quickly through it.

"Dear Mr Rayburn," it read. "Further to our telephone conversation, I am sending two of our pupils – William Baker and Julian Clements – to talk to you about your work in the entertainment industry..."

He was proud of what he'd written. It had an authentic ring to it, he thought.

"Right," he said to Nathan. "You know who you are?"

"What?"

"Your name! Who are you supposed to be?"

"Oh. Yes. I'm Henry Clements..."

"No, no. You're *Julian* Clements..."

"You said I could be Henry."

"Well, you can't. I've typed it all out now. You've got to be Julian."

"Well, all right, but you did say..."

"Look, it's not important. Just remember who you are. Julian, Julian, Julian."

"OK, don't get steamed up."

"I'm not steamed up, Nathan, you are. You look all stiff and tense."

"I am stiff and tense."

"Well, relax. Try to look natural."

Nathan wriggled his shoulders and let his mouth droop open.

"On second thoughts," said Graham, "go back to looking stiff and tense. Come on."

He switched on a smile and walked up to the woman in the glasses.

"Excuse me."

"Picture's started," she said without looking up from her knitting. "Both pictures've started."

"We haven't come to see a film."

"And you're not eighteen, are you? I can't let you in without proof."

"We don't want to get in."

She set the knitting aside with a sigh.

"So what do you want?"

"Ah. Well. We've got this letter –" he explained, waving it in front of her.

"My name's Julian," said Nathan.

"– this letter about a project we're doing..."

"I don't know what you're talking about. Do you want to go in or not? Because if you do you've got to prove you're eighteen. Are you?"

Nathan gave Graham a sideways look.

"I don't know," he said. "I'm Julian, you see, and..."

Graham cut him off with a jab from his elbow.

"No," he said. "We're not eighteen, but it doesn't matter because we haven't come to see a film. We've come to talk about our project. Haven't we, Julian?"

He turned, smiling, to Nathan who had fixed the woman with a panicky grin.

"Haven't we, Julian?"

Nathan blinked and looked round.

"Oh. Right. Yes, we have, Graham. We've come because of our project..."

"William."

"What?"

"I'm William."

"Yes. That's right. He's William and I'm..." His eyes glazed over for a second. "... I'm Julian."

The woman stood up. She was surprisingly tall. She leaned across the popcorn and snatched the letter from Graham's hand.

"Mr Rayburn?" she said.

"Yes," said Graham. "It's a letter from our school. They spoke to Mr Rayburn on the phone, see, and he said we could come and talk to him. Didn't he mention it?"

"No."

"Oh, that's odd. He said if we just brought a letter. You know, a letter of introduction, saying who we were ..."

"Julian," said Nathan. "Julian and William."

"... he'd chat to us. You do know Mr Rayburn?"

She looked at them over the top of her glasses. They had wings like knives, like knives attached to the wheels of a warrior queen's chariot. Graham tried to swallow. The possibility that Beth's father didn't work there suddenly seemed very real. They'd talked about it, but not enough. They should've planned in more detail. They shouldn't have put his name on the letter...

"I know him," said the woman, and Graham closed his eyes with relief. "But he doesn't work here."

"What?"

"He doesn't work here. And he didn't work here when your school supposedly spoke to him on the phone."

She held out the letter between her thumb and finger for Graham to take.

"Oh, dear," he said. "Maybe Mr Protheroe got it wrong..."

"Mr Protheroe?" said Nathan.

"Yes. You know, Julian. Mr Protheroe, who set this up."

"I reckon he did get it wrong," said the woman, folding her arms. "Or someone did."

"So Mr Rayburn doesn't work here?"

"Not any more."

"He did, though?"

"He did. Once. He was our projectionist."

"Where is he now, then?" Graham asked casually.

"Why?"

"Well ... I mean, it's curious, isn't it? Mr Protheroe writing to him and ... and..."

"Very curious. But you don't want to talk to Mr Rayburn. You want to talk to someone who works here. So it doesn't matter, does it?"

"Not really, but..."

The woman held up both hands like someone stopping traffic.

"But nothing," she said. "Mr Rayburn used to work here. He doesn't now. That's it."

"That's a pity because he said he'd talk to us."

"So you said. But he can't now, can he?"

"Do you know where we could find him?"

She pursed her lips.

"I am not at liberty to tell you any more," she said.

"No, no. Of course..."

"You can read, can't you?"

"Yes."

"Well, then. Find out that way. May—"

She stopped abruptly and gave her head a little shake.

"No," she went on. "You want to talk about what a projectionist does, I'll fetch the manager."

Then, keeping her glasses angled on Graham and Nathan, she leaned back and picked up a phone.

"No," said Graham. "It's all right. We'll go back and have another word with Mr Protheroe, I think."

He backed away, stopped, pulled Nathan by the sleeve and then turned and walked quickly out. They hurried down the street, arguing.

"We could've been in deep trouble there, you know," Nathan said.

"Yes, thanks to you."

"Me? It was your idea."

"And it worked, Nathan. Be honest – it worked. Or it would've done if you'd kept your mouth shut. 'I'm Julian. My name's Julian.' Brilliant. Very believable."

"What about this Protheroe bloke, then? Suddenly you're going on about Protheroe and I think you've flipped..."

"Protheroe wrote the letter, you dolt!"

"But I've never heard of him. Who the hell is he?"

"For crying out loud, he doesn't exist. I made him up."

"Well, you might've told me. And all that bother and we don't know a single thing more. We've got nowhere."

Graham stopped walking and thought.

"Yes," he said, "we have. We know he used to work there."

"Big deal."

"And we know he doesn't now. But the key thing is, they don't want to talk about him.

'I am not at liberty to say,' she said. And that means something."

"It means they sussed us out, Graham, that's all."

"No. More than that. She was being very cagey about him. As if he was sacked or something. I'm sure that's what it was. They sacked him. And why?"

"We don't know."

"But we can guess. He's a violent man and he got the sack. The picture fits."

When they got back to the house they went straight to the bottom of the garden to see if Beth had turned up. She had. They found her tipping a bucket of soil onto a fresh mound behind the shed. For a while they watched her jumping up and down to flatten it. When Graham broke the silence by asking her what she was doing, she turned sharply and stared at them with wild eyes.

"Don't creep up like that," she said. "That's not nice."

"What are you up to?"

"I'm making a garden."

Graham flung his bag down in exasperation.

"You can't do that," he said. "You can't just decide you're going to make a garden in a garden someone else has already got."

"There's no harm in it. And I like gardening. Look," she said and gestured proudly behind her. "It's going to be right behind the shed and there's nettles all round so you can't even see it."

Nathan walked up to take a closer look. As far as he could tell it was just a pile of earth with a few stones in it.

"What are you going to put in it?" he asked.

"I don't know yet. I'm just doing the starting bit. The digging and stuff. It's going to be a whassname – a rockery."

"Don't you start heaving rocks around," said Graham. "And I bet you've mucked up the shed as well. Bent forks and I don't know what..."

"No, I haven't. All the tools are in spanking order. I always leave as I find."

She marched over to the shed door and held out her arms to bar the way, a fiery little landowner fending off trespassers.

"It's a bit mucked up at the moment because I'm busy with the garden," she said defiantly. "But I'm going to tidy it up. I left it nice and tidy before, didn't I? Why are you being so horrible, Graham? You ought to be grateful, not horrible."

"You left it *too* tidy before," said Graham. "It's a shed, you know, not a private apartment. It's not your home, you know."

As soon as he said it he was sorry. She didn't answer, just stood there, arms out, staring at him until Nathan muttered something about making tea and moved off. As Graham stalked back to the house, he sensed Beth's eyes probing his back. He barged into the kitchen and slammed the door. Nathan took the kettle to the sink and filled it in silence.

"I know, I know," Graham said. "I shouldn't've said it. But, honestly, first a home and now a garden..."

"I think she's right, though, Graham. No one would know it's there..."

"What are we going to get next, though? A swimming pool?"

"She'll be all right. We'll go down and pack her off in half an hour. See that she's left everything in order."

"She probably will. She's a very determined little thing."

"Meanwhile," said Nathan, "we ought to talk about what's happening tomorrow. The rally, I mean."

"You can leave the rally to me. All you have to do is to make sure people know about it. We want more people at the rally than at the Display of Work, that's the main thing."

"Well, the word's beginning to go round, Graham, but what are you actually going to say?"

"You'll see."

"You've thought of something, have you? Because it could be our last chance before the election."

"You'll see," Graham repeated, then changed the subject. "I wonder what that woman meant," he said airily, "back at the Complex."

"What?"

"When we were talking about Beth's dad and she asked us if we could read. 'Can you read?' she said. And then she said, 'Find out that way.' I wonder what she meant."

"Good point," said Nathan. "At first I thought she meant look him up in the phone book, but I don't think it's that."

He got up and started to pace slowly round the kitchen in the manner of a large wader trying not to disturb fish. Then he stopped and stared at the cooker, tapping his teeth with his pen. Graham watched him, reluctant for the moment to interrupt such deep thinking.

"Well?" he said at last.

"Hmm?"

"What are you thinking?"

"Ah. Have you noticed this before? You tap your top teeth and it makes one kind of sound, but you tap your bottom teeth and..."

"Is that it? You've been striding about like Sherlock Holmes listening to your *teeth*?"

"No. I just got distracted..."

"And I've been sitting here waiting for your pearls of wisdom. Thinking you might've actually worked something out for once in your life."

"I was working something out. Well, not

really *working it out*. More kind of trying to remember what she said, word for word."

He went back to musing and tapping his teeth. Graham heaved a sigh and poured the tea. He could tell when Nathan's musing reached a conclusion: there was a final sharp tap and a yelp of pain.

"Bloody hell," muttered Nathan, staggering to a chair and clutching his mouth. "I just poked myself in the gums."

"Well, it saved me doing it."

"No, really. I kind of jerked my elbow and stuck my Biro right into my gums. Can you see anything?"

Graham turned round with the tea and saw Nathan leaning back in the chair with his lips pulled open and his teeth bared to the ceiling. He looked like a human pedal-bin.

"Is it bleeding? I think I can taste blood."

"No blood," said Graham, glancing into his friend's mouth as he put the tea down. "Only ink."

"Really? Ink? Does it look ridiculous?"

"Not more than usual. Nathan, why did you jerk your elbow?"

"I can't remember now. Yes, I can. I just thought of something else she said. Or, to be precise, what she *didn't* say. She suddenly stopped talking. Remember?"

"To phone the manager, yes."

"No, before that, when she was asking

could we read. She said 'May' and then she stopped."

"May?"

"Yes. May, and then nothing."

Graham drank some tea and looked at Nathan. He had hooked his lips apart with the finger of one hand and was prodding his gums with the finger of the other.

"And you stabbed yourself in the mouth because of this, did you?" Graham asked.

"I didn't mean to. I just thought it might've been, you know, significant."

"No, Nathan. I don't think it is."

Beth in the garden sweating over a rockery which would remain invisible to everyone but her; Nathan in the kitchen trying to rub ink marks off his gums. And we call ourselves the Anti-Noodles, Graham thought.

That evening Dad came home, sank into the armchair and pulled off his boots. Mum was in the kitchen listening to the radio. Toby had sprawled himself on the floor with a comic and Graham was sitting at the dining-room table jotting down a few things he might say at the election rally.

"I've just changed shifts," Dad said to no one in particular. "I'm on lates from tomorrow. I don't mind lates. You know, working through the night."

"Hmm," said Graham.

He crossed out what he'd written and started again.

"Of course," continued Mr Keefe, "you have to sleep through part of the day, which gives you the feeling you're missing things. But I'll be around in the evening. The early evening."

"Hmm."

"So I can spend a bit more time with my happy, smiling kids."

He paused and Graham, keeping his pen poised, looked up from the table.

"That'll be nice," he said and looked down again.

"Oh, yes. Nothing like a good old chin-wag with the offspring."

Dad picked up the paper and flicked it open.

"They're so full of life and they have such interesting things to say. Talk, talk, talk. You can't stop them sometimes. Especially that Graham. Always rabbiting on about something is that Graham."

"Dad?"

"Yes?"

"Are you trying to tell me something?"

"Me? No, of course not. Well, yes, actually."

"What?"

"I don't know. I come in after a hard day's work and nobody looks up. Nobody speaks..."

"I'm busy."

"Right. Don't let me stop you, then."

"No, go on. What were you saying?"

"Nothing," Dad said, rustling the paper. "I just thought it might be a good idea to spend a bit of time together, that's all."

Graham watched the back of his father's head for a while. He found himself thinking about Beth. Wondering what sort of things her father said to her. He pictured her beavering away at the bottom of the garden. Trying to make a quiet, decent place for herself. Entirely on her own.

"It would be good," he said. "You could help me with my lines."

"Lines? What lines?"

"For the play."

"Ah, Shakespeare. Yes, I could do that. I'm not very good on Shakespeare, mind you."

"That won't matter. You'd only have to make sure I was saying them right."

"OK, we'll do that. And then I thought we might get into the garden for a change. Now we're getting a bit more light in the evenings."

"The garden?" Graham said, suddenly alert.

"Yes. It's got very overgrown down at the bottom there. We could make a clearance. I thought we might dig over a patch and put some more spuds in..."

"Down at the bottom?"

"Yes. What do you think?"

"Good idea," said Graham, smiling.

He thought, she won't be able to come if we do that.

He thought, she'll be off my back. Leave me in peace.

And she won't have anywhere to go. She'll lose the home she's been making.

Of course it couldn't have gone on. He knew that. Sooner or later she'd have had to abandon the garden. But tomorrow... Graham hadn't thought that it might be as soon as tomorrow.

What will she do? he wondered. Where will she go then?

EXPOSURE

Friday morning was dull and flat. At the school gates he looked for Beth's head bobbing along among those threading their way in, but he couldn't see her. That wasn't so surprising: she was short enough to miss in most crowds. He'd have to find her later, though. She had to know that the meeting was cancelled. She had to know about Dad's plans for the garden.

He wondered how she'd take the news. Most of the time she was chirpy and irrepressible with a knack of seeing the positive side of things, but he wasn't sure she'd stay chirpy when she heard that the garden – *her* garden – was about to become out of bounds.

The school day, when it started, was uneventful. Slow. Quiet. Everyone seemed to be sitting around like patients in a huge waiting-room. Once, during History, he caught Smith looking at him, but, as soon as their eyes met, Smith turned his attention to his book. While Mr Campbell-Barker droned on at the front, Graham tried to fathom some meaning in that look. Was it the look of someone who was planning something? Or the look of someone wondering whether *someone else* was planning something? He couldn't tell. Perhaps Smith was thinking about his cake. Graham thought about it, too. It was due to take its place in the Display of Work today. What would it look like? Insulting? Humiliating...

"How can we do that, Graham?" Mr Campbell-Barker was saying.

Graham switched his attention instantly from Smith's cake to ... to what? What was he supposed to be doing?

"Well, sir, it depends..." he began tentatively.

"On what?"

"Depends what you mean."

"Depends what I mean by what?"

"By what you just said."

"And what was that?"

"How we can do that, sir."

"We could go on in this circular fashion all morning, Graham. Why don't you simply ask me what I was talking about? Clearly you weren't listening."

"Sorry, sir. I just tuned out for a second."

"Quite. So?"

"Sir?"

"What was I talking about?" said Mr Campbell-Barker rather more heatedly.

"I don't know."

"Ask me, boy, ask me. That's what I just said, isn't it?"

"Oh, I see. What were you talking about, sir?"

"I was talking about History, you may be astonished to learn. How can we hear the authentic voice of the past? I don't mean reading what some historian says he *thinks* went on. I mean what the people to whom it was happening said. Authentic voices."

"Ah," said Graham. "I see. Well, there's recordings, I suppose..."

"A hundred and fifty years ago," drawled Mr Campbell-Barker, making mock pummellings to his head.

"No. Perhaps not. Well, then, let me see ... diaries..."

"Yes."

"Letters..."

"Yes, yes. Go on, go on. The excitement is tremendous."

"And there's ... there's..."

Newspapers.

"Newspapers, sir."

Newspapers. You can read it for yourself. I'm not at liberty to say any more but you can read, can't you?

Graham felt a tingling in his arms and down

his back. Was that what she'd meant, the woman in the glasses? Mr Rayburn doesn't work here any more. But you can read about it ... read all about it ... in the papers.

The local paper. Man Sacked After Attack On Film-Fan.

Check the local paper.

"Keefe!"

"Sir?"

"You've tuned out again, haven't you?"

"Sorry, sir," said Graham. "I'm with you now."

But he remained tuned out for the rest of the lesson.

During the break he dashed off to see Nathan. He found him in Yard Two with his hands in his pockets, muttering to someone about the forthcoming rally.

"Well, I can't say *too* much because it's kind of under wraps until lunch-time..."

Graham pulled him aside and, in something of a rush, told him about the discovery he'd made in history. It was rather more of a rush than Nathan could cope with.

"I don't get it," he said. "Newspapers? Where do newspapers come in?"

"It's what the woman at the cinema said. 'You can read it for yourself.' She meant in the papers. It's obvious when you think about it."

"Not to me it isn't."

"Well, it is to me. Where can I get hold of back numbers of the local papers?"

"School library. But what are you looking for, exactly?"

"Any reference to a Mr Rayburn. How he came to lose his job. Anything."

"It's worth a try, I suppose," Nathan said, stroking his chin. "I'll come with you."

"No. There's something else you can do."

"What? I'm not going to have to pretend to be someone else, am I? Because, to be honest with you..."

"No," said Graham. "It's dead simple. Just listen, will you? Have you seen Beth this morning?"

"Not this morning, no."

"Then see if you can find her. Tell her not to come round after school today. Dad's going to be there."

"Right."

"She'll have to go somewhere else. Until we can get a few things straight..."

"You got a minute, Keefe?"

Anthony Dawkins was walking towards them, head tilted back, looking at Graham down the length of his superior nose.

"No," said Graham over his shoulder. "I'm just on my way to the library..."

"It wasn't a question," drawled Dawkins. "I'm telling you. You've got a minute. To see about the costume."

"Now? Right now?"

"Now. Mrs Backhouse has got a bloke in to take a look at it and sort it out. You have to report to one of the practice rooms in the Music Block."

"The Music Block? Why?"

"Because it's private, dork. Unless you want to be seen wandering about..."

"I don't have to put it on, do I?"

Dawkins leaned closer and gave Graham a confidential punch on the arm.

"Don't worry," he said. "I'll see the coast is clear. Actually, to be honest, I felt sorry for you, having to wear that thing. I thought you were jolly decent to go through with it. You know, for the sake of the play."

He smiled, his head still angled back as if he were posing for a fashion shot. It wasn't an unfriendly smile, though. Graham thought briefly that it was really the nose that made him look so superior, and he probably couldn't help that. He shrugged at Nathan and followed Dawkins across the yard, walking backwards part of the way so he could call out a final reminder.

"Don't forget, will you? Find Beth."

Graham slipped into the practice room and there was the costume waiting for him on the piano stool. He looked round to make sure he couldn't be seen. There was a tiny window, high up in one wall, and a thin strip of frosted glass in the door. Through this he could see the dark blur of Anthony Dawkins' back as he kept watch outside. It all seemed secluded enough.

He began to undress. The room was not designed for disrobing, though, and he had some difficulty bending without banging his head against the top of the piano. It was sound-proofed, too, so he was conscious of a close silence all around him and his own breathing. As he was climbing into Caliban's dishcloth, he struck a clashing chord on the piano with his left buttock, and his heart leapt with fright. Dawkins' face appeared at the frosted glass.

"What are you doing in there?"

"Nothing, nothing. Nearly ready."

I hope this doesn't take long, he thought. I've got the rally to sort out, and those news-papers to look at...

There was a click and the Dawkins' nose appeared round the door.

"Come on," he said. "They're waiting."

"I thought you said they were coming to the Music Block."

"What? Yes, I did. Only they're in one of the other rooms. You ready?"

"Yes. Is it all clear out there?"

"Not a soul. Don't worry. Once they sort your costume out you'll be fine."

Graham took a breath and stepped through the door. The corridor was gloomy but blissfully quiet and empty.

"And Graham," Dawkins said, still holding the door handle. "I meant to tell you, I think you're doing a great job with Caliban."

"Really?"

"Sure. I didn't know you had it in you."

"Thanks. I think Prospero's good, too. You've got the right sort of manner for him, if you know what I mean."

They stood for a moment, smiling at each other, a little embarrassed. Then Graham cleared his throat and asked where Mrs Backhouse was.

"Last room. End of the corridor," said Dawkins with a nod.

Graham padded gingerly down the corridor until he reached the end, but he could see no more practice rooms. No more doors of any kind, in fact, apart from the one which led outside. He turned to ask Dawkins for further directions and was surprised to find him right at his shoulder.

"There aren't any more doors," Graham said.

"That's right. Only this one."

Dawkins leaned across him and opened the door. A flood of light came in from outside. He put a hand on Graham's back and gave him a gentle shove. Then, as Graham stumbled over the step, he said in cheery voice, "Well done, Keefe. You've been Noodled."

Graham spun round and saw the door slam shut in his face. Behind him he heard laughter. A wall of laughter. People laughing and clapping. He turned slowly and was blinded by a ripple of flashlights. Cameras. There were red spots swimming before his eyes. As they faded, faces began to emerge from the cheering crowd. Familiar faces. And one face in particular.

"As promised, ladies and gentlemen," the face was saying. "I give you Graham 'Bloodaxe' Keefe, in all his glory!"

Graham stood with his back to the double doors leading to Yard Two. He kept his head down, like a mourner, and stared fixedly at the large cardboard box he was clutching to his chest. He'd gone to some trouble to get it, but now he was wondering whether it was worth it. The box, the rally, the Anti-Noodles – was any of it worth it? He was a laughing-stock. He should find a hole and crawl into it, not hold rallies.

He became aware that Nathan was hurrying towards him in a state of some anxiety.

"You'll have to do something, Graham," he said, flapping his arms. "They're all out there waiting."

Graham knew that. He could hear the buzz

of the crowd behind him. If he looked over his shoulder he knew he'd see a mass of faces, all gawping at the doors and waiting for him to appear. The Grand Anti-Noodle Rally. Of course, they weren't there to hear about the Anti-Noodles. They were there because the word had spread.

Did you hear about Keefe? Dancing around the Music Block? Stark naked? Someone took pictures apparently.

"Shall *I* go and have a word with them?" Nathan offered, shifting nervously from foot to foot.

Graham took a breath and turned round. His face was pale and shiny.

"No," he said. "That wouldn't be fair."

"But if you're not well..."

"No, Nathan. I'll have to go out there and face them. If I don't, it'll only be worse later."

He wiped his brow with the back of his wrist and stepped slowly towards the doors, seeming to hear the rattle of drums that takes a man to his execution, but actually hearing Nathan drumming on the box with his fingers.

"What's this, Graham?"

Graham half turned and looked at him blankly.

"What's in the box?"

"Sort of ... election material," Graham said grimly.

He pushed through the doors and paused on

the top step that overlooked Yard Two. The sight of him caused the crowd to fall silent almost at once, and for a second or two he stood there, taking in the mass of faces lifted up to him. He saw Angela, and George Marriott and—

"Ooh, look, he's fully dressed!"

Yes. Of course. Peter Smith.

There was a surge of laughter and Graham felt his cheeks begin to burn. He set down the box and held up his hands for silence. The laughter increased.

"What's in the box, Keefe?" Smith called above the noise. "Your latest costume?"

"If you'll all shut up a minute," Graham shouted, "I'll tell you!"

His words came to him as if from inside his own head, a thin, cracked whine which fell feebly against a wall of laughter. He saw Smith pushing through to the front of the crowd. Heard him call out clearly: "He's quite right! Let's hear the voice of reason and sense!" Then, looking over his shoulder at Graham, he added, "And do try to keep your trousers on, Keefe."

Another burst of laughter, and then the noise subsided, as if by common agreement, and everyone turned expectantly in Graham's direction. He was slightly thrown by the suddenness of the silence, and, for a while, could say nothing. Then, tentatively, he began.

"Look, I just wanted to have my say. I don't mean anyone any harm – that's not what the Anti-Noodles are about. Anyway, next week you're all going to choose between us and the Noodles..."

"Noo-dles! Noo-dles!" George began to chant.

"Let the poor boy finish, will you?" urged Peter Smith.

"All I wanted was the chance to tell you what we stand for," Graham went on. "We live in a free country, don't we?"

"A free country?" shouted a boy at the back somewhere. "With parents like mine?"

Graham ignored him.

"We are young," he said, his voice wavering but a little louder. "We are the future. The world can be what *we* make it, what *we* want it to be. What the Anti-Noodles say is, let that be something *good*. Don't let people think we've given up, that we don't *care* about anything!"

He stopped and looked at the rows of faces in front of him. His mouth was dry and he tried to swallow before the jeering started up again. He choked a little in his hurry, but no one jeered and the faces remained fixed on him, waiting for his next word.

"We do care," he declared and he waved one arm in a sudden dramatic gesture. "And if the world's going to change, we – you and me

– are going to have to change it. It's easy to laugh at people, but it's much harder to *make* something – a contribution to life! Making things is what the Anti-Noodles believe in."

"Who'd want what you can make, though?" Smith asked, half grinning at the crowd.

"Well, that's a fair question," Graham agreed, and he stooped to pick up the cardboard box. "Who, indeed, would want what we can make?"

He lifted the box and held it over his head.

"This is what the Anti-Noodles have been doing over the last few weeks!" he announced. "So you can judge for yourselves."

"What is it?" shouted two or three people from the crowd.

"It's Art! It's something that *adds* to the world! The Noodles would have you believe that we are dull, but this –" presenting the box to the crowd in a wide sweep, like a magician – "this has come from our imaginations! It stands for creation and not for destruction. It may not be brilliant, but it is something that we ... have ... *made*!"

Again he paused – he was beginning to enjoy himself – and set the box carefully on the top step.

"So what is it?" Smith called, and Graham ignored him.

"In a minute we're going to put this in the

Display of Work with the other things," he said, almost softly, "and you can see it in all its details, and every time you go by you'll think, Someone *created* that. *That's* what it means to be an Anti-Noodle."

"Rubbish!" Smith was shouting, and the next moment he'd joined Graham on the top step. "A load of arty rubbish!"

"No it isn't!" Graham shouted back. "And mind where you're treading: it's rather fragile, you know..."

"Oh, dear," mocked Smith. "Is it? Do pardon me."

Looking Graham straight in the eye, he jerked his knee up, held it there for a second, then shot his foot through the top of the cardboard box. The crowd sucked in a single breath and several hands flew to mouths.

Graham looked down at the crushed box with Smith's leg still in it. Then he stepped back, gestured towards Smith with both hands and made a little bow – the magician at the end of his trick. Smith looked puzzled. He removed his leg from the box and peered at it. It was streaked with something white and sticky. Cream, was it? Or custard? And were there fragments of coloured icing in it somewhere? The sort you might find on...

"My cake," he said in a harsh whisper. "You *stole* my bloody cake!"

"No, Peter, I only borrowed it."

"My cake! My own bloody cake!"

And that seemed like a good time to make himself scarce, so, after bowing one more time to the stunned crowd, Graham backed into the corridor and shut the double doors behind him.

Let's see how the vote goes now, he said to himself with satisfaction.

An hour later, Graham and Nathan were sitting in the school library. They were huddled in a corner, waiting for the librarian to bring them the back numbers of the local paper. Nathan, however, was beside himself with admiration for Graham and the Anti-Noodle Rally Triumph, and had little time for the local paper.

"But I thought you were so *down*," he said, shaking his head.

"I was down."

"Practically ill, you know, after the humiliation of that costume thing..."

"Yes, quite."

"I mean, more or less naked and all those cameras going off..."

"Yes, OK, Nathan. I'm trying to forget it."

"But I really thought you were so *depressed* you could hardly go through with the Rally at all."

And Graham had been depressed. He had passed from the deep red embarrassment and shame of the Music Block Incident to the golden triumph of the Yard Two Rally – in next to no time. Life, he thought, was rich and strange. Now, of course, he was feeling on top of everything. There was no problem, as far as he could see, that did not have its solution.

A woman brought a pile of newspapers and dumped them on the table in front of him.

"Keep them in order," she said, looking down at the pair of them with vague suspicion. "And don't be too long with them."

"So how did you manage it?" Nathan asked when she'd marched back to her desk. "I mean, how did you get the cake, and how did you know that Smith would squash it?"

Graham took a newspaper from the top of the pile and began to flick through it.

"The cake was easy," he said. "They'd just put it out on the display tables and I told them Smith wanted to pipe his initials in the corner, so they found this nice box for me and I took it away. But, of course, I didn't know he'd jump on it himself. I *hoped* he might, but I couldn't depend on it."

"What would you have done if he didn't?"

"I had an alternative plan up my sleeve."

Graham raised his eyebrows over the top of the paper at Nathan.

"Are you going to help me with these newspapers, Nathan," he said, "or just sit there asking questions?"

Nathan took the next paper from the pile and licked his fingers to turn the page.

"Right," he said. "Yes. What are we doing, exactly?"

"Looking through for anything about Beth's dad. The word 'Rayburn', or anything about the Complex."

"Right. Good."

He frowned at the paper and for several seconds they sat in silence, rustling over the odd page.

"Anyway, what was it?" Nathan asked eventually without looking up.

"What was what?"

"Your alternative plan."

"Oh," said Graham, "I thought if Smith didn't crush the box, I'd do it myself."

"Brilliant," said Nathan, shaking his head again and smiling. "It's the coup de grace and no mistake."

"It did go down rather well, didn't it?" Graham said. "I must say, I'd love to know what the Noodles made of it. I mean, when we hear from Beth..."

"From Beth?"

Suddenly Nathan tensed. He put the paper down and spread his fingers over the table, like a pianist waiting to play.

"Yes," said Graham. "From Beth. Why? You did give her the message, didn't you?"

"Yes, Graham, but I meant to tell you – only

with the excitement of the rally and everything..."

"Tell me what?" Graham said.

"About Beth. Because it was rather weird. You know, the way she took it when I said about your dad going down to the shed..."

"So how did she take it?"

"Well, she kind of panicked. Came over all worried and jittery. She didn't say a word. Just kind of ... left."

"Left? You mean, she left school?"

"Yes."

"Where was she going? Home?"

"Maybe. No. No, I don't think so. She was going in the wrong direction."

"To the shed! She's going to the shed. Before Dad starts going down there."

"What, in the middle of the day?" Nathan asked.

Graham chewed his lip and thought for a moment. Then he tapped the pile of papers on the table.

"It is odd," he said. "But maybe the reason for it is in here somewhere."

So, for the next twenty minutes, they focused on their trawl through the papers. Headlines and photographs flickered before them – flower shows, an open day at the fire station, a footballer cutting a ribbon in a supermarket, big dogs with small cats sitting on their heads... Graham wondered briefly how the paper might report today's events:

WILD NUDE RUNS AMOK IN MUSIC BLOCK!!
See photo spread on pages 3, 4 and 5...

"This is going to take ages," Nathan said, interrupting his thoughts. "There's so much stuff here, Graham. I've just read two columns on a man who lost his teeth on the bus..."

"You don't have to read it all, you fool."

"Well, I got sidetracked – it was kind of interesting – and we don't really know what we're looking for."

"I told you – anything about the Complex or..."

Nathan pointed out that they were only *guessing* that the woman had meant them to look in the newspapers, and that, even if they were right, they had no idea *which* newspaper because there were tons, literally tons, of them...

"Well, what else have we got to go on?" Graham snapped. "The woman hardly said anything else. In fact, she stopped herself, if you remember. She said, "Maybe you can..." or "Maybe it's..." Which is not much use, is it?"

"Actually it wasn't 'maybe'," Nathan said. "It was just 'may'."

"Oh, well," Graham cut in sarcastically, "that makes all the difference, doesn't it?

Anyway, how can you start a sentence with 'may'?"

"I don't know," said Nathan irritably. "Don't carp on at me..."

"May the force be with you?" Graham mocked. "Or, May I take this opportunity to...?"

Nathan stood up, so quickly that Graham flinched.

"No," he said, trying to click his fingers. "Not 'may' anything. May. Capital *M* May."

"The month?"

"Yes. That's what she meant. He left the Complex in May!"

They looked at each other and then dived at the pile of remaining papers like dogs at a stack of straw. The last one was dated January of this year. Too late. They went back to the librarian. Could they see last year's newspapers?

No. Last year's newspapers were on film. If they wanted to see them, they'd have to know how to work the machine.

Yes, yes, they insisted, they knew how to work the machine.

The librarian pursed her lips and set off, slowly, to fetch the film. Nathan, his interest in their quest now re-animated, made silent gestures of frustration at her back and mimed huge kicks to her retreating buttocks. Eventually, however, the film was brought and they were left to stare into the machine and scroll through dense pages of print. Words blurred past their eyes, miles of them it seemed. Ten minutes went by. Fifteen minutes. More...

Then Graham caught sight of it. A name, jiggling up in the right hand corner.

"Rayburn."

He stood up and leaned closer. Nathan moved next to him. His chair scraped noisily over the floor. Graham brought the name to the centre of the screen.

"Derek Rayburn, 42, a projectionist at..."

He saw the headline above it.

Wiped his mouth.

Looked at Nathan and read it again, slowly.

"Oh, God," he said softly. "Oh, my God."

"Prison." Nathan said. "Her old man's in prison."

IN THE DARK

Graham didn't stop running until he reached his gate. His chest heaved and air scraped into his lungs in great gasps. He looked up and saw that the curtains were drawn in the front bedroom. Dad was still sleeping.

All the way home the pieces had been falling into place – the bustle and industry down at the shed, the door wedged shut, the earth in the wheelbarrow, the floor swept so clean, and the rockery. It wasn't a home that Beth had been making – it was a tunnel.

And it was all so mad. She'd have to dig under the road to get to the prison, and she must've known that was impossible. Impossible and stupidly dangerous.

He pushed through the side gate and went into the garden.

He moved slowly now, his arms and legs shaking. A lilac bush blocked his view. He knew that when he walked round it he'd be able to see the shed – but he didn't know what to expect.

One more step and the shed came into view. He'd seen it from this spot hundreds of times. The wooden sides with the green tarpaulin roof, nestled behind the curls of a raspberry bush like some little house from a fairy story.

Now it was different, though. He saw the front wall tilted back, and the door swinging crazily half open. He couldn't see the roof at all.

"Beth!" he shouted, and ran.

He found wreckage. It looked as if a giant fist had smashed the roof in. It had folded like card and the front wall was angled up to the sky. The back wall had been torn away. Long clean nails, twisted and tooth-like, were exposed to the air.

"Beth!"

He had to lean across and haul the door upwards before he could see inside, like someone peering into a cellar. Wood and nails screeched and a puff of dust blew up into his face. When it cleared he saw darkness and a tangle of broken shelves and scattered tools. Rakes and forks criss-crossed in front of him, barring his way. He clambered on to the sloping front, holding himself on all fours over the door-frame. Then he reached in, first one foot, then the other, and let himself drop. He fell further than he meant to. His stomach lurched and suddenly he was in darkness. In a pit. Something had crashed against his knee and for a second he was aware of nothing but the pain. Then he looked up and saw the lawn-mower, suspended just above his head. Only the fact that its handle was trapped under one of the side walls prevented it from falling in on him.

When his eyes were used to the gloom, he saw that the floorboards had been lifted and the dirt beneath gouged away to form an entrance. It was hardly a tunnel really – just the sort of scraped-out space a wild animal might make.

He reached out to move aside an old box and a spade. A sudden groaning sound above him made him stop and flinch. The roof slipped and settled. The lawnmower lurched and stopped. Its blades purred round inches from his head. Soil from a seed tray trickled on top of him. He closed his eyes and shook dirt out of his hair. When he looked into the darkness again, he saw her feet.

Two pathetic little red shoes pointing downwards. Crumpled ankle socks. The bottoms of faded blue trousers. Perfectly still.

"Beth! Are you all right?"

As far as he could tell, the tunnel hadn't crushed her completely. There were pockets of air around her, and the shaft of a broken spade seemed somehow to be holding up a great weight of earth. He took hold of the ankles. They felt warm. He tugged gently and one of them twitched under his fingers.

Thank God, he thought.

"Beth, can you hear me?"

A tiny voice, dark and muffled, answered him.

"Is that you, Graham?"

"Of course it's me," he snapped.

"I got myself stuck, Graham. And I think I went to sleep."

"Don't try to move."

"I'm not. I can't."

He pulled a little harder on her ankles.

"Does that hurt?"

"No, not much."

"Hang on, then. I'm going to pull you out."

This time he managed to move her an inch or two, but he was too stooped to get a proper purchase. When he tried to change his position, the mass of wood above him moaned and the lawnmower blades turned again.

The whole lot could cave in, he thought. It could crush us both. The end of everything. Nothing would matter after that.

He sat down and twisted his feet until they lodged against firm earth. Then he pulled, as slowly and steadily as he could.

"Ow!"

"What's up?"

"I got muck in my mouth."

"Then keep your mouth shut!"

Bit by bit he edged her out of the opening of the tunnel until she was almost crouching in his lap. Her face was pale beneath the filth, her eyes big and round.

"Listen," he said. "I want you to stand up very, very slowly. If you make any sudden movements –"

He lifted his eyebrows and Beth looked up at the lawnmower and the wreckage above them.

"– if you move suddenly, Beth, that lot will come down and I'll get a haircut I don't especially want."

She bit her lip and smiled. Then she stood up and looked around.

"There's a bit of space up here," she said. "If I can just climb up I can crawl out."

"Climb then."

"I'll have to jump…"

"No! Don't jump! Climb on my knees. Use me as a step."

Use me as a step, he thought. That's what she's been doing all along.

He felt her tread on his knees and bit his lip as the pain shot through him again. She wriggled upwards. Her red shoes waggled above him for a moment and then disappeared. Then he stood, and carefully, very carefully, levered himself up. As he did so, the edge of the pit crumbled under his hands and something green and solid jumped straight for him. He arched his back and swung himself up and to his right. The lawnmower handle broke free and whipped past his face. The lawnmower itself crashed into the hole where he'd just been crouching.

But there was no time to take that in. The wall with the door in it was collapsing on him. It fell heavily and noisily, but slowly, and he was able to scramble on hands and knees out of the side of the shed before it fell in with a crack and another cloud of dust and dirt. He rolled onto the grass and stared up at the sky, waiting for the sound to end. Something had soaked the leg of his trousers. He put his hand down and felt the warmth of blood.

He sat up. Beth was sitting a little way off, holding her knees and looking at him.

"Sorry," she said. "I didn't know that would happen."

"You're sorry? Are you really? Well, that's all right, then, isn't it?"

"I didn't mean it, Graham..."

"Don't talk to me. Don't say *anything*."

He dragged himself up and stood over her. She gave him one sidelong look and then buried her face against her knees.

"You know, you're really stupid, you are," he said quietly. "The most stupid kid I've ever seen or heard of."

He felt the back of his throat tighten. It made him want to hurt her. To make her cry.

"Oh, let me join, Graham," he mimicked. "Please let me join. I want to be a spy. I want to be an Anti-Noodle. I'm a clever little thing, I am. And my dad lives in Africa and fights gorillas."

He paused and wiped spit from his chin.

"Africa," he sneered. "I've never heard it called that before."

Then she was looking up at him – still with her arms wrapped round her knees, but staring fiercely up.

"What?" she said. "Heard what called that?"

"You know what I'm talking about."

"How did you find out?"

"We saw it in the paper. 'Local Man Jailed Over Pool Club Blaze.'"

"You should mind your own business!"

"Mind my own business? You're amazing, you are. You smash up our shed and you tell me to mind my own business. It is my business now. It's in the papers. It's everyone's business!"

"But it's my dad!" she shouted suddenly. "And what was I supposed to say? My dad's in prison? Would you have been my friend then?"

"You could've tried..."

"No! You shut up now. I'm fed up with you.

Bossy. Bossy boots. You wouldn't be my friend. You only pretended. Don't think I don't know that!"

Graham blinked. He felt the anger running out of him like dry sand.

"I didn't pretend," he said. "Not all the time..."

"You laughed at me. You didn't care."

"I came here, didn't I? Looking for you..."

"Looking for your precious garden, you mean. Don't make a mess. Don't do this, don't do that. We don't want people knowing she's about, do we? Not her."

"I never said it like that."

"You didn't have to. I *know* what you think. My dad's in prison and your dad's a screw."

"No. It's not like that..."

"It is! You don't want anything to do with people like me."

"Listen, Beth, you joined. You joined the Anti-Noodles. We let you..."

"Big deal. Thank you very much. You think you're cleverer than me, don't you? Well, you're not. The Anti-Noodles were stupid from the start. I never wanted to join them. I was never on your side, Graham."

"No, you weren't. You used me."

"Well, I had to!" she shouted, clenching her fists. "No one would tell me where Dad was. They told me he got a job, but that was all lies.

So I found out for myself. And I don't care what they say about him. He's my dad. He's my dad, Graham. My dad, my dad!"

Her face creased and she began to cry. She gulped air and opened her mouth like a baby bird waiting blindly for food. Her bunched-up nose oozed snot. He watched her for a moment, not knowing what to do. Then he knelt down and touched her shoulder.

"Go away," she mumbled, shrugging him off. "I'm stupid; you just said so..."

"Only because I was frightened," he said. "I was afraid you were hurt ... or..."

"I am hurt. And it's your fault."

She turned to him and swung her hands madly at him, trying to slap him over and over, but he caught her wrists and held them easily.

"You don't want me!" she cried. "I'm not one of your lot. I'm a Noodle! I'm a Noodle!"

He held her wrists until she'd sobbed herself to silence. She fell back on the lawn like a rag and curled up with her back to him.

"Look," he said gently, "you can't stay there. Come inside. To the kitchen. I'll make some tea."

"I can't," she said, quite calmly now but still facing away from him. "They mustn't know I'm here."

He laughed then, in spite of all the tiredness and the confusion still ringing in his head.

"I think they might know *someone's* been

here when they see the shed," he said.

"Oh, the shed," she said, glancing at the tangle of wreckage as if for the first time.

"Look, don't worry about the shed," Graham said. "Let's get indoors."

She let him put his arm round her shoulder and steer her up the garden, though, after a few steps, he found he was leaning against her rather than supporting her.

"What's the matter?" she asked.

"It's my leg, I think. I cut it on something when I was trying to get you out."

"That's my fault as well, isn't it?"

"As well as what?"

"Everything."

When they got to the kitchen he manoeuvred her to the table and took a tea towel from the draining-board. She sat there limply, allowing him to hold the back of her head and rub the towel over her unresisting face. Then he put the kettle on and sat opposite her while it boiled.

"Look, I'm sorry," he said. "For the shouting and everything. I didn't mean all that, you know."

"I was asking for it. That's what Mum always says. Asking for it."

"Look, I don't want to go on about it, but you must've *known* you'd never get to him. A tunnel, Beth? You'd never get him out that way."

She frowned at him and shook her head slowly.

"You still don't understand, do you?" she said.

"What?"

"I wasn't trying to get him out."

"Then what were you doing?"

"I was trying to get in. To see him."

He leaned back in his chair and ran his hands through his hair.

"To get in? But ... but you could *visit*, couldn't you?"

"How? I wasn't even supposed to know he was there. They told me he was working away."

"You didn't know he was in prison?"

"I found out, but they didn't tell me. Some men came to our house one night – men in puffy jackets – and they talked to him in the front room for ages. Then Dad went away with them. Next day Mum and Amanda packed me off to Aunty Sheila's. Just to see her, they said. Just for something nice. But I'm not as stupid as people think. I knew it wasn't for something nice. It was because they took Dad away."

"Do you know what he did?"

Her eyes flashed a little of their old fire.

"He didn't do anything," she said.

"But what do they *say* he's done?"

"You saw it in the paper."

"That business at the Complex? The Pool Club?"

She nodded.

"He told me it was going bust. I used to go down there sometimes, to the bit where they show the pictures. I used to sit with him in the projection room some Saturdays. If there wasn't too much blood and stuff."

"Too much blood?"

"In the films. He wouldn't let me go if the film wasn't suitable."

All those conversations Graham had had with Nathan came rushing back to him – about the brutish father mistreating his daft little daughter. How she needed protecting. And now she was telling him that she used to go to work with her dad; sit with him while the films ran. But only if the films were suitable. Suddenly he felt foolish and very young.

"He knew there was trouble with the club," Beth went on. "They were losing a lot of money, see. Then there was the fire. The place got burned out."

"I read about that."

"The thing is, they pay you if that happens, if there's a fire."

"Insurance?"

"Yes. But when they had a proper look, they found out it was done deliberate. Someone done it on purpose. They said it was Dad."

"Why him?"

"He was the only one there when the fire started. He put it out."

"But you don't think he did it?"

"No," she said, then paused and looked at him. "But it doesn't matter. Even if he did, I still want to see him. He's my dad."

Graham became aware that the kettle was boiling. He got up awkwardly and went over to toss tea bags in some mugs.

"That's why I started the tunnel," she said. "I got the idea when you were having that meeting with Nathan and that girl. I didn't care about the Noodles – I thought all that was daft – but it kept you out of the way. Same as the play. That kept you busy too."

"Is that why you got Mrs Backhouse to give me the part?"

"Not at first. I just thought you'd be good, pretending you had a bad leg and stuff."

He put a mug of tea in front of her and she smiled at him weakly.

"Now you've got a real bad leg," she said. "You don't have to pretend."

"And you really thought you could dig all the way under the road and into the prison grounds?"

"No. I suppose not, really. I took up the floorboards and dug some earth out. But there was tons more than I thought. After a bit I knew it wouldn't work."

"But you carried on?"

"I stopped thinking about it going wrong. I wanted to see Dad, that's all. I didn't know how he was. I kept thinking about him on his own in there. And maybe he was ill or something. So I had to dig. I had to do it because there wasn't anything else I *could* do."

The kitchen door opened with a soft click and Graham's dad stood there, tousled and blinking.

"What's going on here?" he said. "Who's this?"

Mr Keefe made himself some tea and sat at the kitchen table with them. He was unshaven, and he wore a pair of baggy old tracksuit bottoms and his pyjama jacket. Beth stared at him under a deep frown, as if she were trying to picture him swinging keys in the prison where they kept her father locked away.

Mr Keefe sat quite still while Graham told him the story. Once or twice he looked at Beth, but he asked no questions, said nothing, merely listened. Eventually he stood up, walked thoughtfully to the sink and tipped the dregs of his tea away. He rinsed out the mug, concentrating on the task as if it were the only thing in the world he had to do. Then he turned to Beth.

"Look," he said carefully. "In the first place, don't worry about the shed."

"That's what Graham said," Beth mumbled. She took a deep breath and shuddered.

"I wasn't worried about it till he mentioned

it," she went on. "But I am now and I'm very, very sorry..."

"These things happen," said Mr Keefe.

Which was not true, of course. These things did *not* happen and would probably never happen again. But Graham knew what he meant, and what he was trying to say. Mr Keefe rubbed his chin and looked at Beth. He dragged a chair over the tiles – the way Mum hated – and sat next to her.

"There's ways and ways of going about things," he said. "One way is to try and dig a tunnel under a busy road. Another is to go through the proper channels."

Beth gave a tiny groan.

"Don't worry," he smiled. "The proper channels can be pretty effective if you know what you're doing. And I generally do know what I'm doing, don't I, Graham?"

Graham had his leg cleaned and dressed at the hospital. They gave him a couple of stitches and an injection. When the nurse asked him what he'd been doing he said he'd been mucking around.

"That's all. Just mucking around."

He didn't go back to school on the Monday and he turned up late on Tuesday, so he didn't see Nathan until he got to the Humanities room. He got there five minutes early and sat looking blankly out of the window. His leg was numb and tender and the rest of him felt the same. He was vaguely aware of people filing in and talking. Then Nathan dropped into the seat next to him.

"What happened to you?"

"I cut my leg."

"Really? How?"

"Oh, you know. An accident. You know how these things happen."

"Anything to do with Beth? Only the last I saw of you, you were running off home to see if she was there..."

"Yes," said Graham. "To do with Beth."

"And was she there? Because I tried to phone but couldn't get anyone all weekend. And no one phoned me, of course..."

"She was there. And I didn't phone because ... look, I'll tell you later, Nathan, all right?"

"But I don't know *anything*," Nathan pleaded. "I know something's been going on but—"

"Later," said Graham. "I will tell you later. Change the subject."

Nathan glanced sideways at his friend. It was the briefest of glances, but long enough to tell him that changing the subject was a good idea.

"OK," he said. "New subject. I think we're on a dead cert here, Graham."

"Dead cert?"

"The election. Since that business with Smith's cake..."

"Oh, that."

Graham shrugged. The cake business seemed so far away now – distant and unimportant.

"You really turned things round there, you know..." Nathan chuckled.

He stopped short because Smith had wandered in and was standing just inside the door. He looked round the room, saw Graham, then pointed at him and sauntered over.

"I was looking for you on Friday," he said, slinging his bag on a desk as he passed. "We were all looking for you."

"I'm not surprised," Graham said. "It was a stupid thing to do. I'm sorry."

"Sorry?" said Smith, slightly taken aback. "Sorry? You think you can get out of it just like that?"

"I'm not trying to get out of it. If you think you have to pay me back, then pay me back. I'm finished with it."

Before Smith could answer, Miss Garden came in bristling with energy.

"As I'm sure you're all aware," she said, swinging round to face them, "we have reached the day of our grand election. The Noodles and the Anti-Noodles. Voting time."

She wrote the two names on the white board, tossed the marker on her desk and said, "Responsibility or irresponsibility? The path of reason or the way of silliness? I hope I'm not misrepresenting you, Peter."

"Not at all, Miss," Smith said as he sat down. "Silly is what we are. Silly is what we want others to be, while we're still young enough to enjoy it."

"In that case, I'm going to ask the two leaders of the parties to make their concluding remarks. Would Mr Graham Keefe like to begin by speaking on behalf of the Anti-Noodles?"

Graham linked his fingers and looked at his desk for a moment. The room became quiet. He didn't get up.

"I've changed my mind," he said eventually in a quiet but clear voice.

"Really?" said Miss Garden, taken aback a little. "This doesn't sound like the cut and thrust of political debate to me."

"I just think that if you do things the sensible way, sometimes not much gets done. Maybe it's worth having a mad dream now and again. So, I think the Noodles might be right. It's worth a try, anyway."

"What are you doing?" Nathan hissed in his ear. "You're throwing it all away."

"I'm sorry, Nathan. I just can't see the point any more. Sorry."

"Do you mean to say," Miss Garden asked, "that you're giving up? You concede this election?"

"I suppose I do," said Graham.

So there was no vote. Peter Smith's party

was declared the winner, and that was the end of the Noodle Wars. Graham congratulated Smith, shaking his hand and promising to compensate him for the crushed cake. Which left the Noodle-in-Chief feeling rather bemused. He knew that he'd won, but somehow victory had not brought the sense of triumph he'd been hoping for.

Mr Trainor was dozing quietly at the front of the sandwich room when Beth came in cradling a large brown paper bag. She had to open the door with her elbow and enter backwards.

"Oh? You're back?" Nathan said, looking up. "You all right, are you?"

"Yes, thank you very much."

She went to a table near the back and started to delve into the bag, arranging it like a screen in front of her. After a while she peeped over the top and found that Nathan and Graham were looking at her.

"What are you doing right back there?" Graham said.

"Just eating."

"Well, come and eat with us."

"Why?"

"Because it's more friendly. Because you're making me nervous."

"Nervous?"

"All that rustling about. And I can only see

the top of your head. It makes me think you're up to something."

"I'm not."

"Well, that makes a change. Come and join us."

"If you like, then," she said and carried her lunch to their table.

"So," said Nathan as she sat down. "What's been happening, then? Graham told me about—"

But Graham nudged him and he fell instantly silent.

"I'm not going to talk about it," she said primly. "I don't have to, you know."

She plunged an arm into her paper bag and fished out something wrapped in cling film.

"Actually," she said, "I've been asleep a lot. They said I was overtired. Not just tired. *Over*tired. Have you ever had that?"

"Now and again," said Graham.

"Anyway, I got up yesterday and done some baking. Baking's one of the things I'm good at."

She pushed a wodge of cake across the table at Graham.

"It's got hundreds and thousands on it," she said. "And some mixed up with the filling, too. You don't normally get that, you know. I invented that method myself."

Graham looked at the moist brick of cake.

"Is this for me?" he said.

"If you want it. Do you?"

"Of course I do. Thank you. Thanks very much."

"Go on, then. Eat it."

He peeled off the cling film and put a sticky lump in his mouth while she watched.

"Lovely," he said. "I've never tasted cake like it."

"I thought it would be good."

She was watching him with such intensity, like a scientist checking an experiment, that he laughed and spluttered crumbs over the table.

"You don't like it," she said instantly.

"No, Beth, I do. I really do."

"You just spat it out."

"Only because you're watching like that..."

She wiped the crumbs away with her sleeve and put another block of cake in their place.

"If you really like it, then," she said with a nod in Nathan's direction, "you can give some to him."

Graham put the cake ceremoniously in front of Nathan, who unwrapped it solemnly. As she watched, Beth took a biscuit from her bag and posted it sideways in her mouth. It stretched her lips, making her look a little frog-like.

"Well, then," she mumbled through the biscuit, "there's something I have to tell you. I won't be here on Friday."

"No?"

“No. I’m going on a visit. To see someone.”

“Really?”

She tapped the side of her nose and winked.

“And I’m going through the gate, Graham, not underground. Through the proper channels, if you know what I mean. Just thought you’d like to know.”

And perhaps it was only the biscuit, still lodged in her mouth, but she seemed to be smiling broadly.

MONKEY
Veronica Bennett

"Hey, Pritchard! Monkey-features! Monkey, monkey, monkey!"

By teenager Harry Pritchard's own admission, he's a dork. At school he's taunted and bullied by the vicious "Brigadier" Gerard Fox; at home he's weighed down by the chores his mother sets him – the worst of which is having to look after his irritating little sister, Emma. At least, that *was* the worst until Mum volunteers him to visit a severely disabled patient of hers, Simon Schofield, two evenings a week. She says it'll do him good. But how can being a helpless cripple's monkey help him end Brig's bullying? Or get him a part in the Drama Club play? Or win the attentions of beautiful Louise Harding, the girl of his dreams? Simon, though, turns out to be quite different from what Harry imagines and, after meeting him, Harry's life undergoes dramatic – and traumatic – changes!

Touching, perceptive and thought-provoking, Veronica Bennett's book is a first novel of outstanding assurance and quality.

MY LIFE AS A MOVIE HERO
Eric Johns

In times of crisis, Owen Royston Barron is a hero.

Well, in the interactive movies that run in his head he is. In real life he feels more like a worm. "Look after Mum," his dad said – and what did Owen do? He encouraged Mum to move in with slobby, loud-mouthed Frank. Now Owen is out on the street with his mum and wonders if he'll ever be able to get things straight. Will he always be two people – one inside, one outside? Can he ever redeem himself for what he's done? As absorbing and entertaining as the best screenplay, this is the story of Owen's struggle to bring the movie that is his life to a happy ending.

GROOSHAM GRANGE
Anthony Horowitz

"There's something nasty going on at Groosham Grange..."

David Eliot's new school is a very weird place indeed. New pupils are made to sign their names in blood; the French teacher disappears every full moon; the assistant headmaster keeps something very chilling in his room... There are many strange questions to be answered. Most important of all, how on earth can David get away – *alive*?

"One of the funniest books of the year."
Young Telegraph

"Hilarious ... speeds along at full tilt from page to page." *Books for Keeps*

JOHNNY CASANOVA
Jamie Rix

Johnny Worms is hot to trot, the unstoppable sex machine, Johnny Casanova... Well, so he believes. So when love's thunderbolt strikes in the form of Alison Mallinson or a beautiful vision in purple what can Johnny do? And is it his fault that Cyborg Girl, Deborah Smeeton, finds him irresistible?

"A genuinely funny book, sparklingly well-written." *The Independent*

"The first chapter had me laughing aloud at least three times." *The Scotsman*

THE CHANGING FACE OF
JOHNNY CASANOVA
Jamie Rix

"Oh Bosie,
You're rosie,
You're peaches and cream.
You're ice in a bucket
With Oysters Supreme."

Johnny Worms, alias Johnny Casanova, is back on the luv trail. His face may have changed a little – well he *is* fourteen – but underneath he's still the same romantic fool. He's hot to trot for new luv adventures – and he doesn't have long to wait. On the first day of the new school year, Bosie Cricket cartwheels into Johnny's life and puts his heart in a spin! Athletic, gorgeous, sophisticated, Bosie inspires Johnny to verse and song ... but will she give him a snog? Could this be the *real thing* for the unstoppable luv machine? One thing's for sure, farce and hilarity are never far away with the exploits of Johnny Casanova and his crazy family!

LONE WOLF

Kristine L. Franklin

Three years ago, following a family tragedy, Perry Dubois and his dad left the city and moved to a remote cabin in the American woods. Here in wolf country, they lead a solitary life. Perry doesn't even go to school, spending much of his time with his dog, Rhonda, in the cave that's his secret hideout. Then Willow Pestalozzi and her large family move into the empty house nearby and Perry finds his world invaded. For Willow is full of questions – questions that remind Perry of everything he's tried so hard to forget. She wants to be friends, but Perry doesn't need anyone, does he? He's a loner like the wolf he hears howling in the woods. And yet there's something about the Pestalozzis, with their mess and noise and warmth, that draws him in...

Kristine L. Franklin's absorbing and touching story reveals how learning to laugh again also means being able, at last, to cry.